BASH and the Pirate Pig

BASH and the Pirate Pig

story by BURTON W. COLE

illustrations by TOM BANCROFT

B&H
PUBLISHING GROUP

Nashville, Tennessee

Published by B&H Publishing Group
Nashville, Tennessee

Dewey Decimal Classification: JF
Subject Heading: FARM LIFE—FICTION \ COUNTRY
LIFE—FICTION \ CHRISTIAN FICTION

1 2 3 4 5 6 7 8 • 17 16 15 14 13

For Melissa, forever Daddy's little girl.

Acknowledgments

Silly String party wishes to the kids in Clubhouse 206 of the American Christian Fiction Writers—Debbie Archer, Leigh DeLozier, Kate Hinke, Shellie Neumeier, Dawn Overman, Chris Solaas, Cynthia Toney, and Heidi Triebel. Your critiques, encouragement and playfulness are awesome.

Thank you to literary agent Terry W. Burns for adding me to his corral, B&H Kids editor Dan Lynch for inviting Bash and Beamer over to play, illustrator Tom Bancroft for the hilarious depictions, and developmental editor Jamie Chavez for reeling me in when the words drifted astray.

I tip my farm cap to Mom and Dad—the real Frank and Patti—my siblings, and the whole collection of aunts, uncles and cousins who inspired these tales—and lived through quite a few of them.

To my wife, Terry, thank you for putting up with these kids spilling out of my keyboard and wreaking havoc all over the house. You are wondrous.

Praise God from whom all blessings flow, including the blessings of laughter and imagination.

—Burton W. Cole

Contents

Chapter 1

Sentenced to the Farm of Doom

For stupid reasons that weren't my fault, I was tried, convicted, and sentenced to a summer with my wacko cousin Bash on the Farm of Doom.

We live in Virginia Beach, next to the Atlantic Ocean. I hate the ocean. It's full of waves, giant turtles, sharks, and other scary stuff. No, thanks. Give me a bag of chips—the big sack, sour cream and onions flavor—and a stack of comic books any day.

Dad shot down my sensible plans. "Raymond, you're not going to spend another summer lying around on the couch."

I rolled over, careful not to squish the chips, and refastened the button that popped on my Darth Vader pajamas. A corner of my comic book flapped into chip dip. I licked it off so the pages wouldn't stick. "But, mmm, I'm reading. Don't you want my mind improved?"

Dad grimaced. "Not when Peter Porker's the teacher."

"*Parker*. Spider-Man is Peter *Parker*."

I poked my glasses back up my nose and set the chip dip on the floor. Dad picked up the dip and set it on the coffee table. "Look, son, you need to climb trees, run across open fields, and see nature."

Chills shot up my spine. "No! Not summer camp! You have to make roosters out of macaroni and hike blindfolded with a partner who runs you into a tree."

Mom stepped into the room and took Dad's arm. "This is much better. You're going to spend the summer with your cousin Sebastian—I mean, Bash—on Uncle Rollie and Aunt Tillie's big, beautiful farm in Ohio. Isn't that wonderful!"

When a grown-up works that hard to convince you it is, you know it isn't.

"Not the Basher. He's a weirdo!" My face scrunched up thinking about it. "He's always playing tricks. He eats bugs and wrestles pigs and creates idiot inventions that'll cut your ears off."

Mom clucked her tongue. "Raymond, you're always exaggerating."

"No, I'm not. Aunt Tillie has that crazy eye tic flapping

all the time. And Uncle Rollie's always saying strange things like 'scarcer than hens' teeth.' Chickens don't have teeth. The one that nearly pecked my toes off and ate them for lunch the last time we were there didn't, anyway."

Dad chuckled. "Ol' Roly-Poly Hinglehobb says some silly things, but we always had a hoot on the farm when we were kids."

Mom sighed. "Tillie needs you to keep track of Bash, maybe keep him from parachuting off the barn roof with bed sheets tied to his bicycle again."

"Just because I'm eleven and a half, I gotta babysit a dippy doofus who just turned eleven and acts like he's seven? Don't you like me anymore?"

Mom tilted her head. "Your birthday was in February and this is June. That's not exactly eleven and a half."

A dopey haze clouded Dad's eyes. "Laughing Brook up there in northeast Ohio is such a nice, quiet little place."

Oh, no, he's not getting me with this one. "Laughing Brook isn't even on the map. I looked once. You know—to prove to Bash he didn't really exist."

Dad arched an eyebrow. "How'd he take the news?"

"He told me to clean my glasses because both he and Laughing Brook were there."

Mom waved a hand. "Oh, they have a lot of those little places. The names belong to towns that used to be there a long time ago."

"It's still not on the map. It's not safe going to places even Google can't find. Can't I just play baseball instead?"

"We tried baseball last year. You sat in the outfield during the games and read comic books."

"Nobody ever hits the ball to right field. That's why they put me there."

Dad crossed his arms. "Scotty Rodgers did."

"That doesn't count. He's on my team. I'm not supposed to catch balls he hits."

"You aren't supposed to still be sprawled out in right field when your team is batting."

"Going to the farm will be fun!" Mom used her birthday party voice now. "You'll have grand adventures. The fields, the woods and streams, the cows and chickens and pigs. The tractors. Don't you just love tractors? And the sun lightens your hair to such a lovely shade of brown. It's so pretty with your hazel eyes. Oh, you'll have such a wonderful time."

Yuck. What do you expect from parents named Frank and Patti? Everything's a picnic when you're named after hotdogs and hamburgers. I'm surprised they didn't name me Cole Slaw.

Mom knelt next to the couch. "Your father and I have been praying about this for a couple weeks now. Were you not listening at family prayer time?"

God again. Mom and Dad said I wouldn't be so grumpy all the time if I paid attention to God. Ha. I wouldn't be so grumpy if they'd stop pushing me to read that boring old Bible. Besides, I prayed at suppertime.

I looked away. Yeah, I got the message. Because I'd rather sleep on Sundays than go to church, because I hated baseball, because a bug-eating cousin needed to be babysat, they were shipping me off to a stupid farm in stupid Ohio. It wasn't fair.

Mom's eyes moistened. "Raymond, we want what's best for you." Dad squeezed her hand.

Case closed. Sentence passed. I would serve one summer of hard labor at a farm with messy animals and cousin Bash, my third cousin twice removed, but not removed far enough for my safety.

Chapter 2

They Tip Cows, Don't They?

"So, what do you do for fun around here?" I fidgeted on the extra bed crammed into Bash's upstairs bedroom. Racecar curtains flapped about the open window in the coolish, mid-June breezes. The old farmhouse smelled like attic furniture and dust, mixed with damp leaves and molasses. The wooden wall clock chimed an hour way too early to be packed off to bed.

From the other bed, Bash propped himself up on one toothpick arm and grinned that idiot grin of his. "Well, we get up at five-thirty in the morning to start chores. That's when we get to round up chickens, chase pigs, and wrestle with cows."

"Can't wait." I mashed my ears deeper into the pillow. It didn't work. I could still hear Bash.

"I'm working on some new designs for rafts to float on the duck pond. I'm going to catch some field mice and frogs to train as the crew. I've nearly got ol' Gulliver J. McFrederick the Third broke in as a riding hog."

I looked up. "Gulliver J. McWhat?"

"McFrederick the Third. Farm animals either have tags with numbers or long, boring names on registration papers that sound stupid. So I make up my own. Gulliver's a pure-bred Duroc hog."

I flopped back onto my pillow. "I used to have a dog. I called him Spot. A mutt, I think."

"Boring." Bash blew strands of messy blond hair out of his eyes, which practically sparkled blue when he got excited. Which was most of the time. "My dog's name is Uncle Jake O'Rusty McGillicuddy Junior. He's an Irish setter."

I knew I shouldn't ask but I did anyway. "What happened to Jake Senior?"

"Isn't any. Junior sounds cooler than plain, ol' Uncle Jake O'Rusty McGillicuddy."

I shuddered, and not just from a deranged cousin. Spooky stillness lay across the farm in a hush. No sirens wailing in the night. No cars honking or jets roaring overhead. No people shouting.

I listened again. Crickets whirred and brrred. Night birds and monsters hooted and howled. Dogs barked. Bullfrogs burped. All of it in the dark with no streetlights. Not silent.

Just spooky. I pulled the blanket up. The night air suddenly felt cold.

Uncle Rollie had called it a small farm: "Only two hundred twenty acres, give or take a mud puddle."

Small? My whole neighborhood and part of the next one would fit here. An army of sheds, barns, silos, hutches, fences and pens cluttered the place, some packed in clusters and others flung about like a bumpkin giant had tossed aside his toys. Fields of hay, corn, oats and I-don't-know-what-else surrounded it all. A creek flowed out of the woods and curled about the place like a crazy snake made of water.

What I didn't see were any store lights shining the promise of Slushies or Snickers bars.

Major boring.

"Yippee. And I suppose next week we can tip over the cows or something."

"You can't . . ." Bash paused. Sheets rustled as he scooted around in his bed. "Oh, yeah, cow tipping! You city kids don't get to do that very often. Yeah! Um, so whatcha know about cow tipping, Ray-Ray Sunbeam Beamer?"

I winced. He didn't have to make up names for me too.

"I heard somewhere that what you farm kids do for fun is sneak up on sleeping cows and give them a push. They crash onto their sides like trees being chopped down. It's supposed to be funny to watch, especially if you get several lined up in a row."

"Oh, it'll be funny, all right." Bash whipped off the covers. "C'mon, Beamer, it's a perfect night to tip cows. Let's start your summer off right."

Maybe if I tipped just one cow to show the Basher I wasn't a complete loser like him, he'd leave me alone. Besides, it had to be better than staying in bed when I wasn't tired, listening to a birdbrain cousin who wouldn't stop chirping.

We didn't bother changing out of our pajamas. We just pulled on our sneakers. Bash creaked open the bedroom door and we tiptoed along the hallway, though I didn't think cows could hear us coming from that far away. We slipped down the stairs and out the back door. Bash broke into a run, a short madman with flyaway straw hair and sneakers.

We beat along the lane to the pasture where the herd of milk cows slept. They already lay in the grass like a pack of black-and-white boulders. Had Aunt Tillie and Uncle Rollie beat us to it and already tipped over all the cows?

"There," Bash whispered.

One big ol' cow ambled from beneath a tree. She looked to be a long block of angles and bulk—like the trailer on a semi— balanced atop legs that looked a little too long and a little too skinny. No wonder cows toppled so easily. Any kid with a Legos set could build something more stable than a cow.

She lowered her nose to the ground and came up munching a wad of grass. "Do you think she's sleepwalking?" I whispered. I studied the cow some more. "Why are her eyes still open? Are sleepwalkers supposed to look awake?"

Bash tugged at my sleeve. "C'mon, Ray-Ray. Follow me."

He shimmied beneath a barbed wire fence and popped up just inside the pasture. I grunted after him. The sleepwalker's big eyes remained open, staring vacantly toward a thistle patch. She kept chewing though the grass was gone.

I tapped Bash on the shoulder. "Do cows dream? She seems to be in the middle of one that's taxing her brain."

He cupped his hands to his mouth and whispered back. "It's perfect. She won't notice us. Wanna tip her, city boy?"

No, I didn't. "Um, okay, sure."

"On the count of three, Beamer. We'll run at her as fast as we can and smack right into her side. She'll splash right to the ground."

I glanced again at the massive sleepwalker looming through shadows and moonlight. "Will it hurt the cow?"

"Trust me, Ray-Ray Sunbeam Beamer, even as big as you are, it will be like she didn't feel a thing. Okay, get ready. One. Two. Three. *Go!*"

We took off like shots. I outdistanced Bash and I knew I'd hit the cow first and knock her over all by myself. Ha! Tease me for being a city kid, will you? I'd knock this cow over so fast they'd know I'd learned all I needed to know about farms and let me go home.

I kicked up an extra burst of speed. *Boom!* I blasted right into that side of beef. *Wham!* One second—upright. That very same second—toppled. Sprawled out. Flat-on-the-back down.

As I lay there flat-on-my-back down in the dew-dampened grass, staring at twirling stars way up past the still-standing-and-dreaming cow, I slowly realized the ringing in my ears sounded a lot like the Basher gasping with laughter.

"That was, har-har-ha, that was, hee-hee-mrmmph, that was *great*. I've never seen anyone bounce his belly so far off a cow's belly. Belly bumper cars—*awesome*."

I tilted my head up as far as I could so I could see Bash way behind me. "Why are you still back there? I thought we both were running."

"What, and rob you of your moment of glory? No way. C'mon, get up. I'll coach you."

As I began crawling to my feet, I eyed the black-and-white tank on hooves. Her belly bulged more than I thought. A bony plate jutted out like a rear wing at her hip. Good thing I didn't crash into that.

I tried to shake the cobwebs from my head. "Bash, maybe we ought to go back inside . . ."

"So you're just another city chicken boy?"

"No. But . . ."

Bash's arms slashed the air in a demonstration of moves. "Whatcha need to do, city chicken boy, is to run your shoulder into her front shoulder. You gotta chop her at her weakest points, those skinny legs. High center of gravity, you know. C'mon back here and get ready for another charge."

I studied the cow again. She appeared not to have noticed us. I stumbled back to where Bash stood. He grabbed my shoulders and shook them. "It's easy, Beamer. Unless you're too scared."

"I'm not scared." *Well, maybe a little.*

Bash demonstrated his moves on a pretend cow. "Just charge at that front shoulder. Maybe you'll want to lean in a little. Snort a bit too. It helps. Lemme hear you snort."

"Snaaaark. Grrruulp."

"Okay, no snorting. Just run as hard as you can. Ready? One. Two. Three. *Go. Go.*"

I'd show Bash what city chicken boys could do. I charged across the field.

Bash shouted instructions. *"Turn your shoulder. Turn your shoulder!"*

I turned sideways and drove my shoulder into that big, ol' cow's shoulder. *POW!* Dropped. Flat on the ground. Again.

I would have preferred lying there for six or seven days until feeling returned to my arm.

But this time, the cow noticed me. Not all at once. She turned that giant head and peered down her long, snotty nose. Drool dribbled from her churning jaw. Her big tongue darted out, slurping at one giant nostril, then the other. She dipped her head and swiped a lick at me. Moonlight glinted off the rounded tips of her cream-colored horns.

I scrambled to my feet and backed away. "Bash?"

"Yeah, Beamer?"

"I thought only bulls had horns. It's a bull, isn't it?"

Bash hooted again. "What a city slicker. Cows have horns too. Lots of farmers take 'em off. We leave 'em on."

I started breathing again. A cow. Not dangerous. Maybe not. Still, pretty stupid to let something that gigundous to keep her horns.

The cow jumped. Pranced, really. She bounced and skipped and kicked, thundering toward me. I turned and dove through the fence. Halfway through, I remembered it was barbed wire. One metal point tore away my pajama sleeve and another would have ripped away my back pocket if pajama bottoms had back pockets. I felt a breeze where there shouldn't be one.

The cow galloped to the edge of the fence, stopped and bellowed. *"Mmmwwaaaaaaaa! Mmmwwwooooooo!"*

I lay panting, scratched and bruised, but safely outside the pasture. Inside the pasture, Bash rolled on the grass, laughing so hard he barely could breathe. The cow bellowed again. She was laughing too. Those rats! She hadn't been asleep at all.

A booming voice interrupted the mad cackling in the night. "What in the name of Aunt Sadie's beard is going on out here?"

I caught a glimpse of Uncle Rollie before his flashlight beam hit me square in the face. "Ow!" The light darted around until it caught the Basher, now high-fiving the cow on the very shoulder he told me to smash into. "You should have seen it, Pops. Best cow tipping ever. She tipped Ray-Ray twice without flinching."

"Cow tipping!" Aunt Tillie rounded the corner. "There's no such thing as cow tipping. Cows don't sleep standing up and they don't knock over. It's a bunch of foolishness con-cocted by imps like you to harass city folk. Now get out of there and stop upsetting the animals."

The beam from the flashlight traveled back to me. I scrambled to my feet but held one hand behind me to cover the breezy spot.

Uncle Rollie scratched his balding head. I thought I saw a chuckle start to rumble up his belly and bounce his pajama buttons. "Great day in the morning. You weigh, what, all of one hundred twenty pounds, give or take a candy bar? That

Holstein packs about fifteen hundred pounds of solid indifference. How'd you expect to topple her?"

The killer cow still stared at me. I made sure I kept bulky Uncle Rollie between me and the cow on the other side of the killer fence. I tapped around the shredded parts of my pajamas. "Am I bleeding? Eek, don't look behind me."

"Wow." Uncle Rollie admired the barbed wire scratches. "That'll feel better when it stops hurting."

Aunt Tillie and Uncle Rollie marched us back to the house, Aunt Tillie's arms, robe tails, eye tic, and words flapping all the way. "Raymond Boxby, we asked you here to keep an eye on Sebastian. The next thing I know, you're agitating the cows. Worried cows don't milk as well. You dingbats could cost us a couple gallons of milk for every cow you frightened. I thought you were reliable. I need help this summer, not more nuisances. Can't either one of you stay out of trouble?"

Me?

Uncle Rollie shook his head. "Cow tipping."

Aunt Tillie jabbed an elbow at him. "Roland, stop snickering. It's not funny."

"You didn't see the backside of Ray's pajama bottoms, did you?"

I clamped my hands over my rear. As we trudged up the stairs back to the bedroom, the Basher giggled as if he'd seen the finest joke ever played on some schmuck but couldn't let it out because the schmuck would notice. I suspected who the schmuck might be, and I didn't like it.

Back under the sheets, I tried to find a comfortable spot

for my sore shoulder, aching back, and tingling front. What kind of a nightmare had Mom and Dad sent me into?

The bed next to me shook. "Hey, Ray-Ray Sunbeam Beamer, you ever hunt snipe? We've got some big ones here. Really great. Whatcha do is we get a burlap feed sack and you take it out into the woods and beat the ground with a club while singing, 'Here, Snipe. Here, Snipe.' And—"

"Shut up!"

"There's the Great Spotted Snipe, and the Candy-Striped Snipe, and the . . ."

I whizzed my pillow at his head.

"Good thinking, Beamer. A pillowcase will be much better to catch a snipe in than a burlap feed sack."

"Go kiss one of your pigs!"

Bash mushed my pillow to his face, trying to muffle the noise of his hysterics. He came up for air. "Cow tipping. I gotcha, Ray-Ray. Boy, did I get you!"

I let him have it. "You're a . . . a . . . a freaky, frog-faced, dum-dum, hairy troll monster. With warts!"

Bash laughed so hard he had to squish the pillow over his mouth again.

"This summer is going to be fun," he finally gasped.

I wondered if snipes ate numbskull cousins. If so, how fast could I catch a snipe?

Chapter 3

Flight of the Flypaper

Aunt Tillie hollered up the stairs. "Sebastian, bag up the library stuff. It's bookmobile day."

I rolled over on my bed and yawned, a Hardy Boys mystery I'd found on Uncle Rollie's shelf still in hand. We'd finished morning chores. "Morning" still felt like the middle of the night. I scratched at one of the itchy barbed wire digs from a couple nights ago and yawned again. "What's a bookmobile?"

Bash glanced from that kids' Bible of his. "It's a library inside a bus. The library building is in the city. For us out here in the country, they took a big, ol' bus, ripped out the seats and filled it with bookcases. They drive the library to us."

"Cool!" Maybe I'd find a tiny bit of civilization after all in this nutty place.

We stuffed a sack full of books to return: fuzzy-bunny and purry-kitty books from Bash's baby sister Darla, a cookbook from Aunt Tillie, a tractor repair book Uncle Rollie'd used, three novels, and some books recorded on CDs.

There were no books for Bash. "I read lots in the winter and at school, but in the summer, I'm too busy. Except for the Farmin' and Fishin' Book. I read that lots."

I knew what book he meant. "Why do you read that Bible? The words are hard and it doesn't make sense."

Bash shrugged. "It's about farmin' and fishin', so I reckon I understand what you don't."

I may not have paid that much attention in church, but I knew the Bible had nothing to do with farming or fishing. It talked about a naked guy in a garden with a snake, a zoo on a boat, a shepherd with a slingshot, and Jesus, who gathered up a bunch of disciples at the sea. Outside of a couple decent stories, like Samson the muscleman whacking people with a donkey's jawbone, the Bible bored me. This further proved that Bash was two pigs shy of a pen.

We dumped the bag of books into a red wagon. Bash let me take the first turn pulling the half mile or so south to Morris's Corner Store and Seed Emporium, where Bash said the bookmobile parked for two hours every other Thursday. "And we gotta stop in at Morris's too. Mary Jane might be working."

I nearly dropped the wagon handle. "Your pesky neighbor, Mary Jane?" Already twelve and turning thirteen in December, Mary Jane acted like that gave her the right to boss us around. December was a long way away and I'd be twelve myself in February.

"Yep. Mary Jane Morris. Sometimes her mom lets her run the cash register. When she does, I like to pile up a bunch of stuff on the counter, have her add it all up, then make her take it off one item at a time while I recount my money each time to see if I have enough yet."

"Don't you know ahead of time how much is in your pocket?"

Bash grinned. "Sure. I do it because it drives her crazy. She told me once that sometimes she gets bored sitting there. I like to help. If she catches me outside the store afterward, she clobbers me. It's really fun!"

I shoved the wagon handle into his hand. "You're weird."

The bookmobile was awesome. Books everywhere—rows and rows of shelves just jammed full. A checkout lady sat at a desk crammed near the backdoor. Bash hauled me back there.

"Hiya, Mrs. Magruder. Meet my cousin Ray-Ray. He's a book nut like you."

She nearly knocked me over with her smile. "Good morning, young Master Ray-Ray. Any cousin of Bash probably is on his toes. What a pistol he is. Don't you just love him?"

She's a book nut, all right. Emphasis on nut. "Um, hi."

Mrs. Magruder shook my hand until it nearly fell off. "Help yourself. We have plenty of books and there's more where they came from."

The adult books bunked on the top shelves and the kids' books stuffed the low ones. I dropped to my knees and crawled along the carpeted walkway toward the front of the bus, reading the titles splashed on colorful spines as I went. The smells of new books, scuffed carpet, and diesel fumes mixed together in an oddly comforting odor.

I pried loose an action book about a guy who could change himself into a giant fly to buzz around spies. I scooted on hands and knees to the next section of bookshelves, nearly at the front door, when I bumped into a pair of broomstick legs poking out of ripped, red tennis shoes.

"Oops, excuse me." I looked up to see whoever belonged to the shoes. The kid hadn't noticed me parked against his shins. He was too busy staring toward the back where my cousin kept Mrs. Magruder bouncing with a list of books Aunt Tillie gave him.

The kid waved. "Hey, Bash."

I swiveled my head in time to see Bash salute. "Hiya, Jig."

The kid took off running to greet Bash. Then he went flying. That's because he still hadn't noticed me. He thunked right into my ribs and flipped over my back. Arms, legs, books and a baseball cap scattered everywhere. One book zinged into Mrs. Magruder's hair, which was piled atop her head like a butter pecan ice cream cone. The book dangled from one of the swirls like a pecan about to drip out. I covered my head against the yelling sure to come. Instead, she laughed. It was belly-shaking laughter.

Mrs. Magruder plucked the book from her ice cream cone hair and read the title. "'I Wish That I Had Duck Feet.' Well, Jig, darling, you missed my big duck feet. Aim lower next time. Slide a slap shot beneath the desk. That would do it." This time she laughed so hard that if anything else had been hidden in the ice cream cone hair, it would have shaken loose in a spray.

Bash hooted and slapped his leg. Twice. "Sorry, Mrs. M."

A skinny girl at the front of the bus snorted.

Bash leaned over the crumpled kid. "Jig, meet my cousin Raymond Boxby. He's the other dork on the floor."

Jig, flat on his stomach, looked over his shoulder at me still crouched on hands and knees. "Hey."

"Um, yeah."

Bash nudged me with his sneaker. "C'mon, Ray-Ray Sunbeam Beamer, help Jig pick up the books while you're down there."

I smacked his foot away. "Stop calling me that. And what kind of a name is Jig?"

"His real name is Jehoshaphat Isaac Gobnotter. His folks named him after his great-grandfather. We just call him Jig. It fits better. And that girl up there snorting, that's Jig's twin sister, Jecolia Athalia Gobnotter. We call her . . ."

"Lemme guess—Jag."

"I was going to say Jackie . . . No, kidding. Yep, you're looking at Jig and Jag. They're only nine but okay for little kids. They live in that big yellow farmhouse a couple places down from us."

Scrawny Jig sported freckles, and hair the color of fire poked from beneath a green John Deere cap. Jag stood just as freckly, just as fire-headed and just as short. She wore a pink play dress imprinted with tiny, purple flowers. When she dove to the carpet to grab up spilt books, the dress swished to reveal long, blue gym shorts underneath.

As Jig scooped books toward him, his eyebrows shot up so far that the bill of his cap raised a couple inches. He plucked my book out of the jumble. "Ooh, you got a book on the Fly Guy. He's cool. I wish I could fly around like that."

Jag snorted. "I'd still catch you."

"Not if I could fly, Possum Girl. Possums just hang there doing nothing." Jig turned to me. "She swings upside from trees all the time. It's why she wears gym shorts under her dress."

Jag snorted again. Apparently, she snorted a lot.

Bash's eyes started to fire up with that awful glow. Mrs. Magruder saw it too. "Oh, you're up to something again, aren't you?"

Bash nodded. "I've got a great idea."

Jig cheered. "Great!"

Jag snorted. "Great?"

I groaned. "Oh, great."

Mrs. Magruder checked her watch, then started sweeping loose papers into desk drawers. "You'll have to tell me what happens when I come next week. My word, they think I make it all up when I tell them about you at the monthly librarians' meeting."

Bash checked out our books, chucked them into the wagon and then circled us around it. "Jig, Jag, Beamer, how much allowance money do you have?"

I threw up my hand like a traffic cop. "Uh-uh, Basher, your mom said no stopping anywhere after we get the books."

"Nope. She said no buying RC Cola at Morris's after the books. We're not going to buy pop. We're going to buy flypaper."

I scratched my head. "What's flypaper?"

Jag . . . well, you know. And jabbed me with the sharpest elbow I've ever felt. "Where'd you get this kid?"

"Ow."

Bash leaned close as I rubbed my ribs. "Beamer, you know those strips of sticky tape hanging in the barn? That's flypaper." He resumed pacing. "We're gonna buy as many rolls of flypaper as we can, then wrap 'em around Jig. He's not very heavy. When enough bugs land on him, I bet the combined flapping of their wings will be enough so Test Pilot Jig can fly."

"Hooray!" Jig squealed.

I threw up my traffic-cop hand again. "That doesn't make sense. Stop pulling pranks. A bunch of flies and moths and things can't lift a boy, even one as little as Jig."

Jag snorted. I flinched in case she'd throw another elbow, but she didn't. "How do you know bugs can't lift a boy? Have you ever hitched a bunch of moths to a wagon? They're strong."

I moved out of elbow range. "Of course not. It would be stupid."

Bash the rocket scientist crossed his arms and stuck his nose in the air so he could try to look down on me even though I'm three inches taller. "If you never tried, how do you know it won't work?"

"Well . . . it just wouldn't. Stop being such a little kid."

Bash put his fists on his hips and stuck out his chest in his best adult imitation. "Grown-ups are just kids who forgot how to have adventures. When you stop having fun, you're grown-up."

"That's not how it works."

"Our Bible memory verse from last week said, *'I have spoken these things to you so that My joy may be in you and your joy may be complete'* (John 15:11). Joy is short for enjoy, Beamer."

I crossed my arms. "I've been stuck with you enough to know that 'enjoy' can break my leg. And that you'd probably enjoy that."

Bash laughed. "You're funny, Beamer. C'mon gang, let's go."

Morris's Corner Store and Seed Emporium smelled like someone had broken open a couple sacks of flour on the floor and never swept it up. Bash, probably. Bare wood floors buckled beneath racks and shelves loaded with bread, cans, cereals, soaps, root beer mix, balsa wood airplanes, baseball cards and something called paraffin, whatever that might be. Out back leaned a small barn where they kept sacks of seeds.

Behind the counter next to an iron cash register, a girl with chocolate curls glared at us with laser blue eyes. Her hands tightened into two scary fists. I'd run into them before on past visits to the farm. Hoo boy, did I run into them.

"Sebastian Nicholas Hinglehobb, I'm telling you right now, I will make you haul everything back—where it belongs, this time—AND sweep the floors, too, if you pull any pranks. I'm warning you—I'm wearing my pointy-toed cowboy boots!"

"Hi, Mary Jane." I think Bash gulped. "Nope, no tricks this time. Okay, everybody, money on the counter. We need all the flypaper this much can buy."

"Small allowance again, I see. All right, that's thirty-five, sixty, seventy-five, a dollar, one-ten, one-twenty . . ."

By the time she sorted through all the change, we had thirteen packs of flypaper, each package containing four green and gray tubes of the stuff. Mary Jane slammed the packages into a paper bag. "So what's up with the flypaper? You didn't take a bath again and your mom has to hang these in your room?"

Jig snapped to attention. "No, I'm gonna fly. Bash said so."

"You do understand that this is *fly* paper, not fly-*ing* paper, don't you?"

Rocket Scientist Bash crossed his arms and shook his head. "We can't share all the secret details of our experiment with you, Mary Jane. Just keep looking up. If our experiment goes right, Jig oughta be soaring overtop your store dropping water balloons on you in half an hour, maybe forty-five minutes. It depends on how fast your paper catches flies." Bash pulled one of the packs out of the sack and studied it. "It's not crummy flypaper, is it? It might take an hour if you're selling crummy flypaper."

Mary Jane clamped her hands to her temples and sighed dramatically. "Oh, Jehoshaphat Isaac Gobnotter, what's little Sebastian talked you into this time? No, don't tell me. All I need to know is if you're aiming water balloons at me, I'm perfectly safe. You're lousy shots."

"Bye, Mary Jane." Bash bowed as we pushed through the screen door, which creaked open and whap-banged closed behind us.

"Don't slam the door!" Mary Jane hollered.

We jammed the bag of flypaper next to the books in the wagon. Rocket Scientist Bash grabbed the wagon handle. "C'mon, let's go to my place. I'll give Ma the books and we can head out behind the barn. Lots of flies back there."

This could not end well.

Chapter 4

The Jig Is Up, Up, and Away

Fifteen minutes later, we began wrapping flypaper around Jig like we were winding garland around a Christmas tree.

Test Pilot Jig spat and sputtered. "Yuck! Guys, watch it around the face. It doesn't taste as good as it smells."

Jag snorted. "I like it around your mouth."

Rocket Scientist Bash swatted flypaper off the tip of Jig's nose. "Leave his mouth, nose and eyes free. He's gotta see to steer and be able to holler back to base."

I grabbed a fresh roll of flypaper. "You know this is crazy, right?"

26

"That's why it's fun." Bash stepped back to study Jig. "Hmm. We better wind a couple rolls around your cap. We want you upright when you fly. Try to get the big moths to land up there."

We wrapped his arms and legs two or three times. We bundled around his belly and over his shoulders. The more we wrapped, the more goo gunked up our fingers. I tried to brush hair out of my eyes but ended up with brown strands stuck to my fingertips. I looked like a werewolf wrapping a mummy.

We conducted our research behind the barn where a mountain of discarded straw and yucky cow droppings attracted a swarm of flies. Big ones. Horseflies, Bash called them. I figured they were called that because two or three regular flies could saddle up one horsefly and ride him around. And there were normal flies, some greenish-black beetles, some sticklike things that looked like sick mosquitoes that didn't bite, and other bugs that did. I didn't brush any away for fear of leaving a bigger trail of goo across my face.

Rocket Scientist Bash held an imaginary pencil over an imaginary clipboard. "Test Pilot Jig, are you feeling any lighter?"

"No. But my head feels funny."

Bash scratched his head with the imaginary pencil. It drew an imaginary idea out of his imaginary brain. "Walk around the pasture a bit. You need more flies. Let's run you through the pigpen. And the chicken coop. Maybe some feathers will help."

Squawking chickens pecked at bugs squirming on the flypaper. Squealing pigs ran a couple laps around their mud pond with the mummy boy. Slowly, steadily, Jig began to darken. More and more flies stuck all over his body, along with a smattering of brown, white, and black feathers, and fifty-two fat, firecracker-sized, green and gray flypaper tubes, one attached to the end of every roll of flypaper. The stuck flies—and maybe Jig too—buzzed wildly. "I'm feeling a little yucky, guys. Am I floating?"

Bash bent over and tried to poke fingers beneath Jig's sneakers. "Nope, Test Pilot Jig, you're still on the ground. I don't get it. By my calculations, you should be at least two or three feet in the air already."

Jig hopped a little. "Maybe the weeds Jag slapped on me are weighing me down."

Jag snorted. "He needed a tail. All birdbrains have tail feathers. Maybe I should pluck one of your chickens."

I couldn't believe those goofballs thought this could work. This was worse than a couple years ago when Bash tricked me into tying blankets around our necks like Superman and jumping out the back of the hayloft—the low side over the mushy part of the ground. I giggled, the kind of giggle that would spew milk out my nose had I been drinking any. "Maybe he needs more starting altitude. If he jumped out the hayloft, I bet the swarm of flies and feathers would keep him in the air."

Idiot! I hate giggling. And how does Bash always catch me up in his crazy schemes?

Before I could yell "Kidding!" Bash pumped his fist in my direction. "Ray-Ray Sunbeam Beamer, you're a genius."

"Um, I might be wrong. I'm pretty sure I am. Let's not do it. And let's not call me that name anymore, either."

Bash paced circles around me. "I probably already thought of it myself but it's hard to hear my brain with all the flies buzzing so loudly."

Jag steered her twin to the hayloft ladder.

He stumbled. "My legs are sticking together."

So she used a couple sticks to guide the gooey Jig as he jumped into the barn and up the ladder-stairs to the hayloft. "Bounce."

"Mmfff," Jig said.

I tried again to stop the madness. "Um, maybe we ought to get your mom to help."

"Nah. She's been trying to get the baking done for the missions meeting tonight at our house. She told us not to disturb her. That's why she sent us to the bookmobile."

"To get some books so we'd read quietly?"

Bash whipped off his baseball cap to shoo a couple more flies toward Jig. "No. Probably to get ideas. The ladies at the missions meeting always ask her if I've tried any new science experiments. Now c'mon, we don't want to miss Jig's awesome first flight."

Jag pushed open the loft door and Jig stood at the edge. Jag swatted at her fly-covered brother with one of her guide sticks. "Start flapping."

Jig tried, but his arms stuck. Flies buzzed angrily. Jag and I used her sticks to pry Jig's arms loose from his sides. He flapped. A couple feathers fell off. Cardboard tubes banged about until they stuck in the goo. The weed tail on Jig's backside flattened against one gooey leg. A panicked toad stuck to his other leg. I'm not sure when he picked that up. And with the loose hay stirred up by all the flapping, Jig began to look a bit like a scarecrow in a baseball cap.

"Am I flying yet? I think I'm flying."

Bash shook his head. "Not yet. Take a couple test hops."

Fortunately, Jig startled an orange kitten thinking about curling around his leg. Instead of getting stuck next to the toad, the kitten scampered away. Good thing, because everyone knows cats can't fly. Toads can't either, but with all the arm flapping, fly buzzing, feather fluttering, and hay pieces poking, I didn't want to risk reaching in there to make a snatch at it. Maybe it was a flying toad. So far, Bash's Ohio had proved to be a pretty bizarre place.

Jig flapped harder. "It's working. It's working! *I'm flying!*"

It looked more like hopping, but maybe he did stay up just a fraction longer than normal. Maybe it could work. Maybe the Basher had hit on an idea dumb enough to actually . . .

"I'm gonna get a running start and go." Test Pilot Jig backed up, then ran. *"Take off!"*

At that moment, Aunt Tillie rounded the backside of the barn to investigate all the commotion. A blackened and buzzing scarecrow flapped furiously above her, firing a toad missile that landed in her hair.

"I'm flying! I'm flying! I'm fly-ooommmph!"

Test Pilot Jig didn't fly. He dropped. Jig splashed down into the manure pile at the back of the barn.

"Not enough flies." Bash shook his head as a shrieking Aunt Tillie dragged Jig out of the mucky mound of straw and other stuff. "I suppose he'll be collecting some more flies now, though."

Jag stomped her foot. "I shoulda thrown him. I coulda aimed him upward."

Aunt Tillie bellowed from below. "Just once, I'd like a missions meeting without the circus!" She said some other things, too, but she yelled so loudly, I couldn't make out the words. I probably didn't want to.

I stepped to the side of the upstairs door and slumped to the floor, my back to the wall. I hoped my heart would start beating again soon.

I think Jig ended up taking forty-seven baths before getting all the gunk and goo scrubbed off. The rest of us only needed a dozen or so. I didn't think the raisin wrinkles would ever come out of my fingertips.

Aunt Tillie expressed rather clearly that flying experiments should not be conducted, and that she would have thought any kid with an ounce of sense and half a brain would have known that. She said a lot of other things too. A lot of things.

Now I leafed through our library books in Bash's bedroom, to which we had been banished for the night. "Does your mom get that annoyed every time you have fun?"

"Pretty much. I never can figure it out." Bash scratched his ear. "Pops snickers behind his newspaper a lot when she

31

tells him. Then she huffs, an' he says, 'I'm laughing with you,' an' she says, 'I'm not laughing.'"

"Maybe she should."

"She is by the time her missions ladies group meets. That's why they come here every month—they say the stories are too hard to believe without seeing for themselves."

I lay back on the bed, trying to get into my book on the Fly Guy. It didn't seem as exciting as it used to be. Much, much safer than life with Bash, but not very exciting.

"Bash."

"Yeah, Beamer?"

"It was kind of fun. Just a little."

"Yep. It always is."

"And stupid, dumb and dorky! And your mom yelled at me like it was my idea. She always acts like it's my fault! I can't believe you got me into trouble again."

"Trouble? You're just learning to enjoy yourself."

"I want to go home. Like I said before, with you, 'enjoy' can break my leg."

"But we'll have so much fun doing it."

I whipped around, glaring at him. "How about if I come over there and break your leg right now?"

"Catch me."

"*Boys!*" Aunt Tillie's voice screeched from downstairs. "*Go to sleep.*"

Bash sank into his pillow with a smile. "G'night, Beamer."

"Jerk."

Chapter 5

Kings on Cowback

Bash's eyes flashed and flickered like a fuse just before the firecracker blows up in your hand. "You know what we oughta do?"

I kicked a scruffy basketball against the barn. "Plaster your ears in peanut butter and plop you in the pigpen as a chew toy?"

Bash scooped up the rebound, dribbled between his legs and spun the ball to me. "No, doofus—but let's try that sometime with you. No, we should ride cows to the ice cream stand drive-through."

I caught the ball and quivered. "We should?"

"Riding dairy cows to a dairy stand—what genius. They'll probably give us free sundaes or something."

The ball slipped out of my hands. "We should?" Four nights ago, Bash told me I could tip cows, which I thought we could. Now he wanted us to ride cows, which I thought we couldn't.

Bash ran a couple laps around me as he babbled. "Clarey's Burger and Cones is only a mile up the road. I'm surprised nobody's thought of it before. They'll probably take our pictures for the newspaper."

I cringed. "We should?" This had to be Bash's worst idea yet.

"This has to be my best idea yet," he hooted.

"I really don't think we should . . ."

But Bash already was sprinting to the pasture behind the cattle barn. *Why did Aunt Tillie saddle me with the impossible job of keeping the little hamster brain out of trouble?*

I gathered up the ball, dusted it on my T-shirt and dropped it into the empty grain barrel we'd rolled outside to use as our basket. I trudged to the pasture. Bash perched atop the wooden fence gate waiting for a cow to wander close enough so he could launch himself aboard her back. I climbed the railings and sat beside him, wondering how to get us out of this mess without me getting yelled at again.

A long, fat, black-and-white cow ambled in for a curious look-see. Bash nudged me. "Get ready, Ray-Ray Sunbeam Beamer, this one's yours."

"Stop calling me that."

"Jump, Beamer."

"No way."

Bash shook his head. "You gotta learn how to have fun, Beamer. All you wanna do is stay inside all day with your dumb comic books."

"I'd be away from you."

He punched my shoulder. "You won't jump because you're a chicken, chicken, city chicken. Fraidy, fraidy cat."

"I can't be a chicken *and* a cat. That's stupid."

"You're a wimperoni macaroni. Mousey, mousey, wimperoni macaroni."

"Am not!"

"You're too scared to jump on a cow's back. You're afraid of fun."

"Am not." I wasn't afraid of fun. I was afraid of broken bones. Mine. Still, what boy turns down a dare? I didn't want to get teased forever.

"Mousey, mousey, wimperoni macaroni rigatoni on fraidy cat and bologna."

That cut it. "Watch me." I leaped. And almost made it. My fingers clawed at the cow's soft, black-and-white hair, grasping nothing. I slid down her rib cage, my nose smooshed against her belly. Cows at close range do not smell like fresh milk. Maybe like a mix of wet grass, dried mud, dog, and a scent I didn't want to think about—but not like fresh milk. I landed on the thousand pin pokes of a thistle, one of the more pleasant things to fall on in a cow pasture. "Yeow!"

What boy who doesn't want to get teased forever turns down a dare? One smart enough to not have thistles up his nose, that's who. When would I wise up to Bash?

"That was great," Bash gasped between fits of laughter. "You're a blast, Ray-Ray. We should become rodeo clowns. You could do that every night."

I pulled needles from my nose. "Shut up."

"You should try to get her to kick you on the way down. That would be even funnier. We'd get lots of people to watch our show then."

Why wasn't I back home with a bag of barbecue chips, sunk deep into piles of pillows on the couch where I could read—safely— the knock-down action of the Batman battling the Riddler? Oh, yeah. Because God and my parents stuck me with this little creep.

I glared at Bash. "I don't see you trying it."

A big ol' cow grazed near the fence, poking her head beneath the bottom strand of barbed wire. Bash whistled. She ambled over like a pokey puppy. He simply threw his skinny leg over her and floated aboard.

The twerp set me up. Again!

"I've been practicing with Lulabelle Liechtenstein Daffodil Lee here."

"Lulabelle Licking whatzit?"

Bash scratched the top of her head between her horns. If cows could purr, she would have.

"Lulabelle Liechtenstein Daffodil Lee. She's a registered Holstein with a really long official name. I call her Lulabelle Liechtenstein Daffodil Lee for short."

"Why do you always give your animals such stupid names? Why not Lisa? That's easy to remember."

"It's not distinguished enough for a good riding cow."

I rolled my eyes. "Weirdo."

Bash grinned down at me. "You're the one sitting in a cow pasture."

Yuck! I popped up and inspected my pants. Nothing but a little bit of mud. Phew.

Fine. I'd show the little showoff. A full-grown Holstein—the black-and-white cows—stands nearly five feet tall at the shoulders, taller than us. But Jerseys—that's what Bash called the reddish brown cows—are a full foot shorter. A little red Jersey stood daydreaming at the other end of the gate.

"That's Daisy Nancelene Kalio Kow," Bash said.

I crept up the boards again, held my breath and gently crawled onto the short cow. She barely shifted. I shuffled about a bit, trying to figure what to hold. I ended up lying along her back, her knobby spine bumping like a row of golf balls into my chest and belly, and wrapped my arms around as much of her neck as I could reach. Cows have big necks.

Bash waved his ball cap. "We're the Cowback Kings. Let's ride 'em, Cowboy King Beamer!"

"Shh. You'll wake her."

"Aw, she's not sleepin'. Watch."

Cowback King Bash somehow steered Lulabelle toward the gate. Hanging from her side, he unlatched it and swung it open. Lulabelle plodded through. Daisy What's-Her-Name woke up and followed.

"Daisy Nancelene Kalio Kow tags along wherever Lulabelle Liechtenstein Daffodil Lee goes."

I didn't want to tag along. But I had no choice. Bash never explained how to steer a cow.

The Basher kicked at the gate. I couldn't see if it closed. And away we lumbered.

Bash perched just behind Lulabelle's front shoulders, holding on to the knob at her neck, steering her with taps of his high-tops just behind her white forelegs. As long as there weren't any interesting weeds poking up, she took direction well.

"Shouldn't we ask your Mom and Dad if it's okay to ride the cows?"

"'Course it's okay. Ma and Pops won't get me a horse. So I ride what's here. They see me ridin' cows all the time. I'm a real *cow*-boy."

I clung to Daisy's neck. "Don't you have any bridles so we can steer these things?"

"Don't need 'em."

I started sliding down the side of beef and had to practically run up the cow's ribs to regain my spot stretched out along her back.

"Ray-Ray Sunbeam Beamer, you gotta lean with the cow, roll when she rolls and bounce when she bounces."

"Stop calling me that and get me some glue."

The cows ambled down the driveway and onto the road.

"Um, Bash, do your parents let you ride cows on the road?"

"Why not? If I'm riding a cow to the backfield, I have to use the driveway to get there, right? So if I'm riding a cow to the dairy stand, I need to take the road. They know that. Duh."

"But they don't know we're riding cows to the dairy stand."

"They let me ride my bike to the dairy stand. A cow's just a big bike without the wheels. C'mon, let's go." Bash grabbed Lulabelle's head by her cream-colored horns and aimed her north. She slogged forward.

"Bash, this is crazy. We can't . . . *oof.*" Daisy hopped onto the road and fell in line behind Lulabelle. Like it or not, I was on my way to the dairy stand. Riding a cow.

We hoofed it more or less in single file, sometimes on the left shoulder, sometimes in the left lane.

Oof. Ow. Oof. Ow. I bumped about the Jersey's back with every rolling clomp of the hoof. Cars whizzed by in the right lane. Oncoming cars swerved around into the right lane, too, with furious honking of horns.

I ducked. "Um, how do we navigate to the other side of the road?"

"Don't be such a city boy. Pedestrians face traffic. The cows are walking, so they face traffic. Besides, it's really cool to get a look at the drivers' faces."

"But we're *on* the road. You don't walk on the road. You walk on the side of the road."

"Well, duh. If we move off the road, the cows would fall into the ditch."

An oncoming red pickup truck almost forgot to swerve to miss us, then just about clipped a sports car screeching the other way.

I buried my face into Daisy's red shoulder. "The ditch would be nice."

"Fine, city baby. Lulabelle Liechtenstein Daffodil Lee, *ho!*" With that, Bash steered his cow in front of a screeching car to the other lane. Daisy plodded along behind.

"Why did the cow cross the road? Because the city slicker wanted to get to the other side!" Bash thought his joke hilarious.

The cows marched along but kept wandering off the shoulder and into the traffic lane as if no one would care. Drivers did.

"Look at that, Beamer. We've got eight cars lined up behind us and another semi's coming. We're making a parade. *Awesome.*"

I peered back. "That guy in the blue car looks kinda mad."

"He's just wishing he'd thought of this great idea first."

He was wishing something all right, judging by the veins popping on his neck. But I don't think it was for a cow to ride.

The cows kept walking. Cars kept honking as they whipped around us, their drivers either laughing or yelling. Mostly yelling. Every time I peeked, I quickly scrunched my eyes again. My arms hurt from clutching Daisy's massive neck. My legs ached from trying to wrap my sneakered toes into her sides.

My jerk-face cousin sat straight, tall, and proud atop Lulabelle, cackling like a madman in ball cap and patched jeans. If I survived, I planned to stuff the little creepazoid's socks full of wriggly worms and extra slimy slugs.

"Look, we're riding on genuine cowhide leather seats. Mine's even two-tone."

"Ugh." I needed to load more than worms and slugs in his socks.

"And check out these dual horns."

I was trying not to get too close to the dual horns, myself.

"Four on the floor!" Bash yelled.

I looked up and snorted. I couldn't help it.

"Automatic flyswatter."

"Cut it out, dork. I'm trying to hang on."

"Four cylinders!"

"Huh?"

"Cows have four stomachs, city slicker."

"Oh."

"And don't forget the onboard drink dispensers."

"Yuck."

I wasn't pelted with poor puns for long. We were about to actually ride dairy cows through the dairy stand window.

Chapter 6

Dairy Drive-Through

The cows clomped up to a building the color of spicy brown mustard. The big front window was framed in ketchup red, while some sort of green splashed around the drive-through window. Pickle, I think. Dill. A big, swirly plastic plop of strawberry ice cream loomed atop the roof, sprouting up behind a sign lettered in chocolate brown: "Clarey's Burgers and Cones."

The jostling of the cow had already set my stomach at odds with the rest of me. The sight of the place nearly finished me off. Did I mention the Swiss cheese-colored curtains? With actual holes.

The ice cream lady didn't take kindly to cows lumbering up to the drive-through window. "If she spills it, you're cleaning it, kid!"

Cowback King Bash bowed from his black-and-white, uh, steed. "We'll have two hot fudge sundaes to go from this colorful castle."

"Look, smart guy . . ." Right about then, Lulabelle poked her pink nose through the dill pickle service window, knocking over two Cokes set out for another order. She pushed further through the window, tilted her head sideways for a better reach and slurped Cokes in big pink swipes of that long, curling cow tongue. She scooped up a couple dozen packs of salt while she was at it.

The lady slapped Lulabelle's snout, trying not to touch cow snot mixed with Coke. "Shoo! Shoo!"

"Mmmooooaaaaawwww," Lulabelle bellowed.

The clerk jumped back, crunching into a stack of cones poking out of a dispenser. Lulabelle casually withdrew her head, munching on a bag of fries she'd snagged.

"I didn't know cows liked french fries."

Bash looked at me like I was a first-grader. "Duh, they're vegetarians."

"Then it's a good thing she didn't chomp that hamburger too."

"Duh, again. Hamburgers aren't made from ham, you know."

"So why call them hamburgers? Why not cowburgers?"

Bash threw up his hands. "That wouldn't make any sense. Tomorrow we can ride a couple of the pigs here, and *then* we can order hamburgers. Just don't get hot dogs. They're not . . ."

"Yeah, I know, not made from dogs. What do they use for fish sandwiches? Owls?"

"Fish, chipmunk brain. Why would they call it a fish sandwich if it wasn't fish?"

"No reason."

Bash shook his head. "Owls. What a nitwit."

While we discussed the menu, the nervous clerk splotched ice cream into two cups, splashed hot fudge on top and shoved the sundaes at us.

"Take them and get out of here or I'll call Clarence."

The Basher tipped his ball cap in a Cowback King salute. "We'll ride our hogs in tomorrow. I've trained my pig Gulliver J. McFrederick the Third and he's real good. Wait till you see!"

"We're closed tomorrow." She slammed the window.

Bash steered the cows toward the picnic tables. "See, I told you they'd be so excited that they'd give us our ice cream for free."

"She was excited, all right."

"But I really thought she'd shoot our picture for the newspaper."

"She wanted to shoot, all right."

Our hot fudge sundaes finished, Bash grabbed Lulabelle's horns like a videogame controller and aimed her toward the road. *"Giddyup."* The cows didn't move.

"Bash, I don't think they understand 'horse' talk."

Bash scratched his head and tried again. *"Milkshakes."*

The store lady threw open a side door and zinged peanuts and M&Ms at us. "No milkshakes. Get lost. *Now.*" She slammed the door.

The cows wandered out of the parking lot, rejoining the stream of honking, angry drivers. At least sticky ice cream hands gave a better grip. At the speed of snails, we swayed, bounced and bumped our way toward home. If I wasn't so busy holding Daisy's neck, I'd hold my stomach. I was going to be sick if we didn't stop soon.

The cows stopped.

A Mustang blared past. A Jeep Cherokee hurtling the other direction slowed to a crawl as a gob of kids leaned out the windows and laughed. A big-haired woman squawked from a tiny Beetle stuck in front of our stuck cows. A red-faced guy in a semi looked ready to push us off the road.

Bash clicked his heels against Lulabelle's sides. *"Milkshakes. Giddyup milkshakes!"*

I groaned at the thought of moving but feared standing still. "Why did we stop?"

"Clover blossom."

"Who's Clover Blossom?"

"Not who—what. See those purple clover blossoms alongside the road? Lulabelle loves 'em. She stopped for a snack."

Daisy dipped her head for a few mouthfuls. I nearly slid nose-first down her neck. The fact that ramming into her horns would have stopped me from kissing pavement was little comfort. "Well, get them moving."

"Have you ever tried to interrupt a cow eating clover? Too bad you didn't bring one of your comic books. You'd have lots of time to read it."

The Beetle lady inched around us, her big hair bobbing like an angry poodle. I don't know the meaning of half the words she barked when she slipped past us but I got the idea.

Cowback King Bash stiffened. "Uh-oh," he whispered.

"I know, but she's gone now."

"Not her. Way up the road—see that car weaving through traffic?"

"What? *What?*" It was the rare thing that could make Bash nervous. This must be bad.

"That looks like Ma's car. I forgot to ask her if we could take the cows out for a walk."

"I thought you said they let you ride the cows."

"They do, on the farm. It's my first time on the road." Bash glanced at the wildly approaching car. "She's probably upset that we didn't invite her along for such a great idea. She could have ridden a cow too."

I gaped at Bash. "You said riding a cow on the road was just like riding a bicycle." How could so much stupid be rolled into one skinny boy? I doubted that being left out of the cow caravan bugged Aunt Tillie one bit.

Bash slid off Lulabelle's back. "We better hurry."

He planted himself behind Lulabelle and pushed. She

didn't appear to notice. He backed up a few steps and ran, slamming into her rear quarter while shouting, *"Milkshake!"* The startled Lulabelle bolted across the road, an orange pickup careening around her. Daisy darted after her, almost slamming into the truck.

Lulabelle hurdled the ditch. Daisy . . . oh, no. *Don't jump!*

Lulabelle landed as gracefully as a blocky, fifteen-hundred-pound steak on legs can, and scampered through the corn, crushing young plants in her wake. Daisy soared after her with me flapping above her like a cape on Supercow.

I thudded back onto my cowhide perch just as I heard a car door slam and Aunt Tillie shriek. "Raymond William, come back here with those cows right now!"

Whether the cows came or went wasn't up to me. Daisy tore after Lulabelle, with me thumping up and down on her back like a kid on a candy rush whomping a drum. I bounced backward until I slid right down her tail. Then a hoof caught me in the stomach. Worse, I lost my hot fudge sundae too.

As I lay there gasping and heaving in the dirt and corn stalks, I heard the Basher explaining his grand plan to Aunt Tillie.

". . . and I had my allowance to pay for the ice cream but the lady gave it to us for free 'cause of how great our idea was. I shoulda remembered to invite you, Ma. You woulda loved it!"

Aunt Tillie didn't. "Hang onto that allowance because it's the last you'll see until you're seventeen. Make that a hundred and seventeen! Now go get those cows. And pull your cousin's face out of the dirt."

That night, after Daisy, Lulabelle and the rest of the herd that had wandered through the open gate were rounded up—nope, it hadn't latched—after apologies were made for half an acre of ruined corn, and after my breath almost returned, Bash and I sprawled across the beds in his room.

Bash snickered. "That was a bad idea."

"No kidding. Your mom yelled like I meant for the cows to crush the neighbor's corn. It wasn't me who thought up riding cows to a drive-through window."

"Not that. That was a great idea."

"Does the elevator reach your top floor?"

"I meant our rodeo act. The dismount where the cow kicks you on the way down didn't come off as funny as I thought. Your idea of smooshing your nose in her side works much better. Do that one again next time."

I heaved my pillow at the cackling gooney bird, then rolled over against the far wall, as far away from Bash as I could get.

"Ya gotta admit, Ray-Ray, we had fun."

No, *we* didn't. I'd get him for this. Oh, I'd get him back.

I hated this place.

Chapter 7

The Tree Fort
and Elephant Hunt

Bash thumped me with the wheelbarrow. "What we need is a tree fort."

I swung the shovel and plopped another load of cow muck into the wheelbarrow. What we needed after a morning of cleaning cow stalls in the milking barn were baths. "Why do we need a tree fort?" As soon as we finished chores, it would be our first day of parole since the cow-riding incident a week ago. *Please don't get us locked up again.*

Morning milking was over and the cows, their bellies full of a breakfast of grain, had returned to the pasture for another day of grazing. We got stuck with the messy job of cleaning up after them every morning.

Bash shook a pitchfork full of straw across the empty stall I'd just shoveled and scraped. "So we can have a secret clubhouse. So we can have brave adventures. So we can scout for elephants and rhinoceroseseses." Bash added a bunch of extra "siss-siss-sisses" to the end of rhinoceros.

I wiped sweat from my brow so it wouldn't slosh around my rolling eyes. "Yeah, right. You get many elephants and rhinos in Ohio?"

Bash ran the wheelbarrow toward the back door to dump the load on the manure pile that Uncle Rollie would spread later on fields for fertilizer. "Dunno. That's why we need a tree fort. You can't spot 'em without a tree fort."

I moved to the next stall and tugged at my jeans. I must not be eating enough. My pants were slipping. So were my brains for even letting Bash talk about tree forts and elephants in Ohio. "Are you and reality ever on speaking terms?"

Bash bounced the now empty wheelbarrow back across the concrete floor. "You got no 'magination, Beamer. You can't have fun without 'magination."

I shoveled another heavy cow pile and slung it into the wheelbarrow. "Just once, I wish you'd think of something real that made sense."

Bash spread more straw. "Just once, you oughta think of something. Anything." He leaned on the pitchfork. A corner of his mouth edged into a crooked grin. "If you'd rather, we could watch for bears."

"Bears?"

"Sure. Black bears wander over from Pennsylvania sometimes."

I moved to the next stall and heaved gunk at the wheelbarrow. Some of it splattered onto Bash's jeans. He was too busy talking to notice. "See, we'll build the tree fort at the edge of the woods and watch for bears. An' elephants and rhinoceroseseses."

"Why?"

"Because we're dry cleaning."

I shook my head. Logic, I get. But my cousin's roller coaster reasoning—I don't even want a ticket for that ride. So why did I keep getting on? "Dry cleaning what?"

"Us, owl breath. The longer we air dry out here, the less chance Ma'll make us take baths."

I'd love to scrub off some of the stink of this farm. But a bath before lunch is a little much for even me. I scraped goop from the last stall and tried to figure it out. Building a tree fort would keep Bash out of Aunt Tillie's sight for a while. And maybe out of trouble. That would keep *me* out of trouble. And me being smarter than Bash would keep him out of trouble. But still . . .

"When's the last time you saw a bear?"

Bash flicked a bedding of straw over the last stall. "Aw, never. Pops saw one last July. Uncle Jake O'Rusty McGillicuddy Junior barked an' yipped an' growled until he chased it away. Bears hardly ever come this far. That's why we need to build a tree fort—so we can spot one. Or an elephant or a rhinoceroseseses."

I leaned the shovel against the wall, where it would be waiting for me after evening milking was over. "Bash, trying to find a bear on purpose would be stupid."

"It's better'n letting a bear sneak up on you."

I squinted at the woods across the field. Not even Bash's imagination could make real elephants or rhinos crash through the trees. But a bear—there was one, a real one, last year. Uncle Jake chased it away.

Once we were inside the house, Aunt Tillie roamed, growling at us to clean, dust, do dishes, and stop making all that racket. When we weren't working, the Basher read his Bible at me as if it were exciting. Maybe a bear wouldn't be so bad.

I scratched my head. "Okay, let's build a tree fort. But what if we see one? Can you outrun a bear?"

"Don't have to. I only have to outrun you. Ha!" And he ran outside.

"Jerk." I trotted after him.

The Basher zeroed in on one of the forgotten, broken-down grain sheds that Uncle Rollie meant to knock down years ago. The problem appeared close to solving itself. The roof drooped so much that it almost met the floor, which sagged in an attempt to get away. Weeds and wheat grew between the buckled floorboards that remained. One wall squished outward while another looked ready to crumple into bed for a nap. What was left of two cement steps up into the shed looked more like chunks of chalk melted by rain. The whole thing smelled like a dirty, wet dog.

Bash zipped up the steps and dashed inside.

"I asked Pops a while back if I could have the door." A big, blue door lay on what was left of the floor. The shed quivered as Bash grabbed the door by its black knob and dragged it toward the opening where it was supposed to be standing. "We can use the old wood too."

"Farms are like giant boxes of Legos for country kids, aren't they?" I poked my glasses up my nose and stared into the shaking shed. "Why a door?"

"For a floor!" Bash hopped to the ground, the door teetering on the edge of the doorway. "Grab an end."

It felt like wood—and left a couple slivers jammed into my fingers—but hefted like cement. We lugged the heavy thing toward the woods, stopping three or four times to rest. We dropped the blue door with a whump in front of a goofy-looking apple tree in a small orchard at the edge of the woods. About four feet up, a thick limb twisted away from the trunk before curling upward. Three other gnarled branches rambled about the first one—the wrinkled hand of an ogre waiting for two elephant hunters to place an old door in its palm. Which, after a great deal of pushing and straining, we did.

Bash pulled off his ball cap and wiped it across his forehead. "It's wedged pretty tight, Beamer. C'mon, we need hammers and nails."

We ran to Uncle Rollie's workshop. "Pops lets me use his tools sometimes. Here, stick these nails in your pocket."

"Maybe we better go back to the barn and ask." Bash clanked through toolboxes and clattered out a couple hammers. "Pops doesn't mind as long as I put 'em back where

I found 'em, Most of the time, he doesn't even know I borrowed 'em."

"That's the part that worries me."

Bash shoved an orange box of nails at me again. "C'mon, we're losing time."

"If you're sure . . ." I emptied two handfuls of long, shiny nails from an orange box and jammed them down my right pocket.

We ran back to the old shed for wood. The pointy tips of the nails scratched at my leg and ripped the bottom out of my pocket. "Yee-ouch!" I howled and hopped and clawed at my leg.

Bash whipped around, nearly whacking me with a couple boards he'd pulled from the shed. "Don't lose the nails."

Too late. A cluster of nails cascaded down my pants leg and plinked around my sneaker.

Bash covered his mouth but I could see him snickering. "Guess you better carry 'em in your fists, Beamer."

We worked at it the rest of the morning. We secured the blue door floor to the tree. We built a wall on the woods side from boards yanked off the tottering old shed. Scrap chicken wire fenced one end while the tree trunk walled the other end. We found a sheet of plywood with a chunk missing for the final wall. We sawed out a few more chunks for lookout windows like in a castle tower. It looked more like a dinosaur with big teeth bit into it. This was better than I expected.

I tugged at my pants. "This is almost fun."

"See? All it takes is 'magination."

We nailed together odds and ends until we had three

stools, a table, and part of a bunk bed. We hung a sign on which Bash had painted *Look Out Fort* with some orange tractor touch-up paint.

I wiped my glasses on my T-shirt and put them back on. "What's the fort supposed to look out for?"

"Not the fort, dork-dork. Us. It's a lookout post so we can watch for elephants and rhinoceroseseses."

I peered into the woods. "And bears?"

"An' bears."

I shuddered. "Seen any yet?"

"Nope. You scared 'em away with your loud hammering."

"You hammered too!"

"I pounded nails in a comforting way. Anyway, we're not looking for bears. We're looking for elephants or rhinoceros- eseses. And I haven't seen any yet."

I stomped my foot on the door floor. "Maybe they only come out at night, like the deer."

Bash jumped off his wood block stool. "Great idea, Beamer!"

"What is?"

"A campout! We'll catch 'em for sure."

"I didn't say that."

Bash paced around the door floor. "I've got a couple sleeping bags in my closet somewhere."

I slumped onto a grain box chair. "I didn't say camp out."

"We'll call Bonkers 'cause he's the best with animals. Have you seen his pet lizards? He's gonna train them to wear vampire teeth and scare the girls."

"I didn't say camping."

"C'mon, Ray-Ray Sunbeam Beamer, let's go tell Ma we're camping out tonight."

"Stop calling me that! I'm not camping out and that's final."

Chapter 8

Lost in the Woods

I shifted my aching rear on the rock-hard blue door floor, the black knob jabbing me in the back. There wasn't much room to move. The door floor in the apple tree next to the creepy woods also held three sleeping bags, one battery-operated lantern, one flashlight, one backpack of snacks, and two lunatics.

The lunatic with straw-colored hair saluted. "What a great idea, Beamer!" Bash.

The lunatic with milk chocolate skin threw a thumbs-up. "We gotta sing camping songs!" Christopher "Bonkers" Dennison.

Bonkers, Bash's neighbor across the woods and best friend—besides me, I mean—kept rabbits, ferrets, turtles, snakes, mice, and a skunk. He wanted to be a veterinarian.

Bonkers threw back his head and belted out a tune that sounded like that dumb song "The Old Gray Mare," only with words far more disgusting:

"Great, green globs of greasy, grimy gopher guts / Mutilated monkey meat / Little dirty birdy feet / French-fried eyeballs dipped in kerosene / And I forgot my spoon!"

"But I have a straw!" Bonkers made slurping sounds.

I held my stomach. "Gross."

Bash scratched his ear. "How about chipmunk tails and blistered feet?"

Bonkers tipped his cap. "Horsey hair topped with piggy breath?"

Bash clutched his stomach like he was trying to keep a belly laugh from escaping. "Chicken snot and vulture beaks!"

I slumped against a fort wall. "You guys are disgusting." Then before I could stop myself, I stirred the stew. "Pimple soup and muddy toes to eat."

Bash held up a paw for a high-five. "Good one."

I snickered. "Axle grease and crabby teacher's teeth."

Bonkers scratched his head. "I dunno . . ."

Bash clipped my shoulder. "Good try, though, Ray-Ray Sunbeam Beamer."

I crossed my arms. "Stop calling me that."

Jungle Bash jumped up and peered over one of the dinosaur teeth cutouts. "Anybody see any elephants or rhinoceroseseses yet?"

Safari Bonkers peered over another window of Look Out Fort. "I saw four wild turkeys coming over here." Safari Bonkers turned to me. "How 'bout you, Wildman of the Wild? See any giraffes or anything?"

I peered through the chicken wire. "A moth. And mosquitoes that don't realize Aunt Tillie lathered us in spray. Mosquito spray must taste like their ketchup. C'mon, get real, guys."

Jungle Bash dug into the backpack. "Time for our zebra and lion sandwiches." A glob of grape jelly plopped onto the door floor. "Careful, they're still oozing blood."

Oh, yuck.

Around us, an army of crickets and other bugs hummed, buzzed, chirped, and crackled. Bullfrogs burped and boinged. Something—a fish, I hoped—splashed in the creek. It sounded kinda big for a fish. It was a fish. Had to be a fish. Fish don't have claws.

I peered through the twilight across the field to where lights shone in the farmhouse. The farmhouse seemed farther away now.

"Can houses walk?"

Bonkers wiped peanut butter on his sleeve. "I don't think so. Why?"

"Just curious."

Bonkers' brown skin faded into the dark. Bash's straw hair kinda glowed, like a spider dancing in midair. I shivered. Bears have sharp teeth. Werewolves have sharp teeth. Creek monsters probably do too. None of us had teeth to match.

"How come we didn't bring Uncle Jake?"

"No room. Besides, he doesn't like the dark. He stayed home."

Smart dog. Wait, what if a bear showed up? Who'd chase it away now? One of the gopher guts in the fort with me? Yeah, right.

I hate the dark. It makes me think of scary stuff. Monsters. Walking houses. Cricket armies. I tried to think about safe things instead, like church, but that was worse. At church, they talk about oogie-boogie stuff like sins and blood and hell and forever torture and being ready to die. Blech. What kind of talk is that for a happy place? I listened to the cricket army plan their invasion. In the morning, Uncle Rollie and Aunt Tillie would find three corpses in the tree fort with cricket teeth marks gnawed on all the bones. Brrr!

Bash inhaled deeply, as if trying to pull the whole night air of horrors into his lungs. "This is so cool! I can't wait to tell the kids in Sunday school all about it."

Bonkers sighed. "We probably could sell tickets to the next campout."

I scooted lower. I was the tallest but if I crouched enough, any diving bats would tangle in Bash's and Bonk's hair first while I escaped. I didn't want the guys to notice so I kept them talking—not a hard thing to do. "How come you like church?"

White teeth flashed from where Bash sat. "It's fun. An' the Bible is about farmin' and fishin'—planting seeds, growing fruits, and harvesting and stuff."

Now Bonkers's teeth shone just below two glowing, white dots that I hoped were his eyes. "Jesus told lots of farming stories. And his main helpers, Peter, James, and John, were fishermen."

Why couldn't we have picked a night with a full moon so we could see the monsters coming? "But church is a bunch of 'Shalt Nots.' Thou shalt not do this. Thou shalt not do that. Thou shalt not have any fun."

Bash's glowing spider hair turned to the woods. I heard a sigh and the spider hair turned back toward me. "The 'shalt nots' protect us. Remember when Ma told us not to ride our bicycles off the barn roof or we'd get hurt? She knew our bed sheet parachutes wouldn't work."

"It would have helped if she'd shalt-notted *before* you pushed me off the roof."

"We didn't ask before."

"Oh. So God's saying become a Christian and nobody gets hurt?"

Bonkers shook his head. "Nope. It's not for sissies. They killed Jesus."

"So what's the point?" What screeched? It better be just an owl. Wait. Do owls eat kids' eyeballs and tennis-shoed feet?

Spider hair turned my way. "To go to heaven, of course."

Bonkers tugged at his cap. "I got scared once. When I was little. But Jesus said, 'I've got this.'"

I shivered. "So does it always get so dark and spooky out here at night? Don't people in Ohio know about streetlights?"

Bash looked up. "Then you can't see the stars."

Safari Bonkers jumped up. "Did you see that?"

I sucked in my breath. "What? Where? How many teeth? We're gonna die."

Bonkers held a finger to his lips. "A fox, I'm sure of it. We gotta follow it. C'mon."

"Why? I'm not moving." But now I sat alone in Look Out Fort. By myself. Surrounded by owls and cricket armies. *"Wait up, guys!"*

Bonkers had the flashlight. We left the lantern at Look Out Fort to mark our place. We crashed through the woods trying to find the trail of the fox—if it was a fox and not a coyote or black bear or worse.

Bonkers huffed and puffed. "Don't lose it. I've never seen a fox's den."

We smacked into bushes, tripped over logs, and bounced off trees—you can't see in the dark. We zigzagged across animal trails and brushed against those little black thistles that look like squished beetles.

It took us ten or fifteen minutes of charging through the dark to do it, but we did it. We lost the fox. Phew!

That was the easy part. We'd also lost ourselves.

Jungle Bash panted. "Say, did you notice which way we came?"

Safari Bonkers scanned the shadows. "I think over here and then . . . no, we came . . . It's hard to see in the dark."

I gulped in three calming breaths. "Maybe you could trying turning on the flashlight."

"Oh, yeah. How come you're squeaking like that?"

"I'm not squeaking!" I squeaked.

Bonkers swung the beam around. Tree. Tree. Tree. Tree. Tree. Tree. Woods! All woods. All around us, woods. And it all looked exactly the same to me.

He scratched his chin with the flashlight, making his face glow like a monster. "Hmm. I don't think I've been to this part of the woods yet."

Bash turned in a slow circle. "I have. But it looks different in the sunlight."

I gulped three more quick breaths to steady myself. "Can sun even get through here? We've probably been lost for hours and hours and hours, and it's noon and we can't see 'cause we're so deep into the woods that the sun can't shine in, and no one can find us even though they're looking and crying and calling for us, and we're lost forever, and they've rented out your room already, and I'll never get off this stupid farm and out of stupid Ohio and back to my room and . . . *Ow! You hit me!*"

Bash nodded. "You sounded like baby Darla."

"If I was Darla, I'd be back at the house in bed sound asleep and not lost in the woods with a bunch of killer animals and two brainless, monkey-meat maniacs . . . *Ow! You hit me again!*"

Bonkers played the flashlight over the mossy ground. "We could sleep out here till morning."

I could hear chomping noises—Bash chewing his tongue to help him think like he always did. At least, it better be Bash chewing. "Nah. I left my sleeping bag back at the fort. Let's just go back."

I stomped my foot. *"But we're lost."*

Bonkers waved the flashlight. "It's a small woods. I've been lost in bigger."

"You've done this before? And we followed you? *Are you crazy?* No, I must be the crazy one. Otherwise, why would I be here?"

"You better slug him again. I don't think you hit him hard enough the first two times."

"Nah, he'll be fine. He squeaks all the time. City kids. Let's go back. But first, let's ask for directions."

I whirled about. "There's a gas station? Can we get a Coke too?"

The flashlight fell on Bash as he looked up into the blackness: "Hi, God, it's me, Bash."

Huh? "Don't you have to use formal names or something? Shouldn't it be, 'O Mighty and Holy Eternal King, I, Sebastian Nicholas Hinglehobb, do solemnly swear . . .'"

"Ray, He knows me. We talk all the time. And even if we didn't, Ma and Pops tell Him all about me. All. The. Time! It's embarrassing. But nice."

Weird. I closed my eyes for prayer.

"Anyway, God, show us the way like You always do. Thanks. You're the best!"

He looked into Bonkers's flashlight beam. "Okay, let's go."

I opened one eye. "That's it? Don't you have to pray for hours and cry and moan and roll around and stuff? That's what some people at my church do when they're in trouble."

Jungle Bash poked from one side of a bush, then the other. "Sometimes, I suppose. But when you talk with Him all the time in the first place, you don't have a lot of catchin' up to do."

Bonkers scratched his ear. "*Don't worry about anything, but in everything, through prayer and . . .* uh, petting, no, pet, pet, *petition,* yeah, that's the word . . . *with thanksgiving, let your requests be made known to God. And the peace of God, which,* um, *surpasses every thought, will guard your hearts and minds in Christ Jesus* (Phil. 4:6–7)." Phew.

Bash slapped a high-five with Bonk. "Wow, Bonkers, that was a long one!"

I bumped into a tree. "Yeah, well, those verses don't say anything about guarding our bodies, and it seems to me that's what's in danger around here."

"Wildman of the Wild, hearts and minds are the hard part 'cause we can't see 'em. If God can guard those, the rest is easy. Besides, they're *His* bears."

"I wish he'd keep them on leashes," I muttered.

"Okay, we were aiming that-away chasing the fox, so we must have come in from over . . . there." Safari Bonkers took the lead, followed by Jungle Bash, followed by the Wildman of the Wild clutching Jungle Bash's T-shirt.

Bonkers burrowed us through some underbrush. "It can be a bit scary."

Bash spit out a leaf or a bug or something. "Singing helps."

I groaned. "More gopher guts?"

"Nope. We're looking for the light. How about . . . *This little light of mine / I'm gonna let it shine / This little light of mine / I'm gonna let it shine . . .*"

Bonkers joined in. "*. . . This little light of mine / I'm gonna let it shine / Let it shine, let it shine, let it shine.*"

We backed out of one almost deer trail and tried another.

"Hide it under a bushel?—No! / I'm gonna let it shine / Hide it under a bushel?—No! / I'm gonna let it shine / Hide it under a bushel?—No! / I'm gonna let it shine . . ."

Didn't we already pass that tree with the hole in it three or four times? We're gonna die and they're gonna find our bodies under that tree.

". . . Let it shine, let it shine, let it shine."

At least bears won't eat us. They'd be frightened off by the awful noise Bash and Bonkers call singing. I decided to join in:

"Won't let Satan (and we blew "Foof!" instead of singing a word) it out / I'm gonna let it shine / Won't let Satan (foof) it out / I'm going to let it shine / Won't let Satan (foof!) it out . . ."

I tripped over a log across the pathway. Did I trip over it before?

". . . I'm gonna let it shine / Let it shine, let it shine, let it shine."

Isn't camp the other way? Well, we've tried two other directions already.

"Let it shine till Jesus comes / I'm gonna let it shine / Let it shine till Jesus comes / I'm gonna let it shine . . ."

Shine! Did I see a glimmer of something? It's the tunnel of light you see when you die. I knew it. The bears already ate us.

"Let it shine till Jesus comes / I'm gonna let it shine / Let it shine, let it shine . . ."

Bash and Bonkers see it too. It's tiny, but it sure looks

bright in this gloom. Now they know we're dead too. Unless, maybe . . . is it . . . the . . . fort?

"*. . . let it shine!*"

It is! Look Out Fort. Our little battery-operated lantern still shines. Let it shine!

"Awesome. Thanks, God!" Jungle Bash yelled.

"I just followed the angel," Safari Bonkers said.

The what?

Jungle Bash ran a couple laps around us. "That was so cool. Let's do it again! Wildman of the Wild, this time you lead. Get us really mixed up. Then we'll find our way out again."

"You guys are crazy. I'm going to the house." I climbed into Look Out Fort and started rolling up my sleeping bag.

Bonkers followed me. "Aw, c'mon, Ray. If you'd stop squeaking, you might realize you're having fun."

I yanked the cinches on the bedroll. "You guys are trying to kill me!"

Bash's head peeked over the door floor. "You won't see the elephants and rhinoceroseseses if you go home."

Good!

"We won't go into the woods," Bonkers said.

"Not till morning at least. But don't worry—God always knows where we are," Bash said.

I squinted into the darkness, trying to spot the house across the long, dark field. It was miles away. I sighed.

"Okay, I'll stay. But only if someone switches places. I can't sleep on the doorknob."

Bash pumped his fist. "Awesome!"

Bonkers pushed the backpack across to me. "We have another zebra and lion sandwich oozing with blood if you want it."

I lay back on the bedroll and took a bite. "You really can see the stars now that the treetops aren't in the way."

Something hooted. Bonkers bolted up. "An owl! Let's see where it goes."

"No way. This little light of mine and I are staying right here."

Then the rain came. Bash flipped his sleeping bag over his head. "I just remembered. We forgot to build a roof. Last one to the house is rotten monkey meat!"

Soaked rotten monkey meat at that. "Wait up, guys!" But they were gone.

Crash!

That better not be thunder and not a bear. I didn't bother looking. I dropped my sleeping bag and ran. I only had to pass one of them.

Chapter 9

A Hayfield of Hope

The sun rose warm and bright. Birds sang. Flowers bloomed. My socks matched.

Rats! I hoped for rain. A thunderstorm. Maybe a nice, friendly tornado.

What lousy luck. We were stuck with the fifth sunny day in a row. It was a perfect day—for disaster.

On unsteady legs, I slumped against the archway into the kitchen. I rubbed sleep crust from my eyes, *yawned*, shook cobwebs out of my head, and tried to ignore the dread bunching up at the bottom of my stomach. Aunt Tillie in pink robe and fuzzy pink slippers stood at the stove scooping pancakes out of a frying pan. Uncle Rollie, in dusty blue jeans and a brown plaid work shirt, sat at the table reading a bulky, worn-out Bible while pouring coffee into a cup without looking. Baby Darla's high chair stood empty since she, being the only sensible one among us, was still asleep.

Leave it to Bash to shatter the morning quiet. He flew down the stairs for morning chores, yelling all the way. "Pops! You get to teach me to bale hay today!"

The spatula Aunt Tillie held over the pancakes clattered to the floor. Uncle Rollie missed his coffee mug, dousing a plate of toast with a hot, brown stream. Darla began wailing from her room.

Uncle Rollie mopped coffee off his toast with the big, red hanky he pulled from his back pocket. "About that, son . . . I said *maybe* we could work on that one day this summer."

"Yeah! Today's a day an' this is summer. When do I start?"

Uncle Rollie started to stuff the hanky back into his pocket, yanked it back out, stared at it as it dripped coffee, shook his head and dropped the hanky onto the table. He sighed. "Look, I've got Rusty Rose and Jerry Strauss coming over at about ten.

"Yeah, but I get to drive the tractor, right?"

"I haven't trained you yet."

"You *promised*."

"That *maybe* I would teach you one day this summer."

"Jig and Jag Gobnotter both drive their dad's tractors an' they're only nine."

Uncle Rollie arched a furry eyebrow. "Yeah, I heard about that. Did Mr. Gobnotter get that chunk of the tractor barn replaced yet?"

"Jig says most barn doors are built too small. Now they can back their baler right in 'cause he widened it. Jig said now that he knows how, he could widen ours too. But I think I should get to do it myself!"

"Our doors are fine." Uncle Rollie rose from the table and let the toast splat back onto the plate. "Listen, champ, I think today we'll let Rusty and Jerry work the wagon with you and Ray. I'll drive. But we'll get to your turn. Don't worry."

"Promise?"

Uncle Rollie raised one of his big, bear paw hands. "Cross my belly button hairs and hope to snort milk out my nose."

The spatula clattered again. "Roland!"

"Well . . . Okay, Pops," Bash said. "Can it be chocolate milk? It'd look funnier."

"Sebastian!" Then Aunt Tillie whirled on me. "And don't you start, Raymond!"

I shook my head. "I don't think I like chocolate milk sprayed out of noses all over my pancakes."

"Get out to the barn, all three of you!"

Bash and I fed cows, chickens, and hogs while Uncle Rollie tended to the milking.

"Pops probably means I'll get to drive the tractor tomorrow." Bash crammed a lot of hope into his voice, but not even he was buying it. The buckets of water and feed seemed to drag his skinny arms below his knees. He even forgot to trip me like he usually did when I carried the water bucket.

Haying season began before I arrived on the farm and Bash had been begging the whole time for a chance to plop his seat into the tractor seat. Uncle Rollie finally told him, "Yep, maybe one day this summer, like, oh, maybe the last of June." Today was the last of June.

As we finished chores, Aunt Tillie stepped onto the back porch. "Roland! Telephone!"

"Coming, Mattie."

I don't know why, but Aunt Tillie always calls Uncle Rollie "Roland," and he always calls her "Mattie." Her real name is Matilda. Nobody in this weird family can leave well-enough names alone.

Moments later, Uncle Rollie was back, shaking his head. "Chickenpox? Both of them? For crying out loud. What are boys their ages doing with chickenpox? And on a baling day."

Uncle Rollie stood next to the tractor parked by the barn and gazed at the field of hay, already mowed and raked into rows like a fat snake coiled into a rectangle maze. Uncle Rollie glanced at the sun. Then back at the hay. He scratched his basketball belly through his plaid shirt and sighed.

"Well, boys, you're both too short to heave heavy bales very high up a hay wagon. If we're going to get this done . . . Bash, it looks like you're driving the tractor."

Bash blasted into the black seat of the orange Allis-Chalmers tractor, and slung a wispy arm over the wheel. "How fast will she go, Pops?"

"Easy, Earnhardt. We don't use road gear in the hayfield. Start her up."

Bash knew tractor basics. I leaned against the corn crib and watched as he clamped his hand on the shift stick, stomped on the clutch pedal with his left foot, threw the tractor into gear, and yanked his foot off the pedal. The tractor jumped like a sick frog, coughed like a sick horse, and died like, well, a sick tractor.

My day just got brighter! *Mr. Know-It-All doesn't know it all. Ha!* I sat on a cement block in front of the corncrib and got comfortable to watch the show. Bash's Irish setter sat at my side and plunked his head across my lap.

Bash tried again. The tractor coughed and quit again.

Uncle Rollie winced. "Let the clutch out easy, champ, easy."

I tried not to laugh, but it was marvelous to see the Basher so perplexed. Plus I didn't know a tractor could turn into an orange jumping frog.

I scratched Uncle Jake's ears. "Serves the joker right, huh, boy? He's always pranking me. The tractor's getting him good."

Uncle Jake sighed.

Bash tried again, easing the clutch out at grandpa speed. The tractor jerked, then ran. Well, crawled. Uncle Jake lay down to take a nap.

Uncle Rollie grinned. "Slicker'n snot on a doorknob."

Gag me.

"Now ease it back to the baler."

Bash looked back, aimed and goosed it. *Clang!* The old red baler shuddered from the crack of the tractor hitch. Uncle Jake whimpered.

"Bash!" Uncle Rollie barked. The twitching muscles in his arms nearly tore his straining sleeves. Uncle Rollie sucked in a huge breath then blew out the air like a leaking bike tire. "Sebastian, this isn't bumper cars. Now pull up a bit and back in *slowly*. When I hold up my hand, stop."

I leaned down and ran my fingers through Uncle Jake's back. "This is the best day ever."

Bash chewed his tongue so hard his left cheek bulged with the effort. If he tried hard enough, he'd gnaw his tongue right off and wouldn't be able to talk. *Score!*

This time, Bash snail-crawled backward but steered wrong. The baler pull bar and tractor hitch were about a foot apart.

I started to laugh but Bash sagged so much, it squished the chuckles back down my throat. He dropped his straw-colored head atop his tiny hands clutching the big steering wheel. Uncle Jake stood up, shook the dust out of his coat, and trotted toward the woods. "Wish I could go with you, boy. This is getting hard to watch."

Uncle Rollie tugged his blue and yellow Kent State ball cap and looked up at the kid slumping so small in the tractor seat. "See that, you're learning. Now you know another way not to do it."

Bash sat up, drove forward a few feet, chomped his

tongue, then turtle-toddled the tractor backward. Better. No frog jumps. But slow. Maybe I could sneak away to make a peanut butter and strawberry jelly sandwich.

Bash eased the hitch bar between the two prongs of the trailer tongue. Uncle Rollie dropped the hitch pin into place. "Finer than frog's hair. Hold it there while I hook up the power takeoff."

Uncle Rollie glanced at me while tugging a long, round bar from the baler and attaching it to a Pinocchio's nose-like gear poking out the backside of the tractor. "The PTO runs the baler mechanisms."

"Oh." I nodded as if I had a clue.

Bash then attempted to back both tractor—which zigged one way—and baler—which zagged the other—to the hay wagon. All three had to be hooked together like a train before we could get under way. Uncle Rollie squeezed my shoulder. "Let's just pull the ol' wagon to the baler so we can start before quitting time."

Wagon hitched, we climbed aboard.

Uncle Rollie waved his arm. "Okay, champ, head 'em out."

———

Bash lined up the baler on the outside loop of the coiled snake of hay. In his best announcer's voice, Tractor Driver Bash bellowed, "Drivers, start your engines!"

"Uh-oh," Uncle Rollie said from where we stood at the front of the wagon.

Bash rammed the gear for the baler into place and popped the clutch. The tractor rabbit-leaped forward and took off.

The force crumpled Uncle Rollie and me backward and we didn't stop rolling along the wagon floor until we smashed against the rack wall at the back.

Uncle Rollie clawed at the rack. "Chicken scratch and porcupine quills! The boy has all the grace of a cub bear in boxing gloves." He muttered a couple other things, too, but I couldn't hear them above the clattering of my teeth bouncing around in my brain.

We staggered to our feet while the wagon bucked and bounded across the bumpy field. My glasses buzzed about my nose and Uncle Rollie's belly jiggled like Jell-O on a go-cart with a square wheel. The baler pounded out a rapid *whir-whir, chunk, whir-whir, chunk* cadence. The tractor swished back and forth with each bump in the field so that sometimes the red baler snatched at the hay with its twirling yellow spoke-teeth, and other times missed it completely.

Uncle Rollie hopped about the wagon, waving his thick arms like he was warding off a whole troop of killer mosquitoes. "Hey! *HEY! STOP!!*" Bash didn't. He probably couldn't hear over the roar of the tractor, the clanking of the baler, and the awfulness of the song he belted out at the top of his lungs: "Onward, Christian tractors, driving as to war . . ."

Big, grinding arms inside the baler jammed and packed the grasses into tightly tied bales that stutter-chugged up the back chute of the baler to the wagon. I dragged them aboard as Uncle Rollie flung his baseball cap at the tractor to get Bash's attention. The wind whipped the cap sideways across the hayfield in a swirl of blue and yellow until it sank into a mound of hay a few rows over.

Man, we better remember to get that thing before it gets baled up into cow food.

Bash kept singing.

Uncle Rollie leaped from the wagon, staggered, then hoofed it, arms flailing, toward the tractor faster than I thought an old man could run. Tractor Driver Bash caught a glimpse of the Creature from the Black Hayfield running in for the kill. "Yipes!" He jerked the wheel and yanked on the throttle to make his escape, but he already had it cranked to full speed.

Then he noticed it wasn't the Creature, but his dad. Bash slammed on the clutch and brakes so hard I splatted across an oncoming bale of hay, which blocked me from sliding headlong into the backside business end of the baler.

Bash cut the gas to the tractor. "Hiya, Pops. I'm doing great, huh."

Uncle Rollie hunched over, hands on his knees, wheezing and coughing. *"Huuzzzz. Heerrrzzzz. Huuuzzzz."* It was the first I knew that he was allergic to hay. He flopped against the tractor's big back tire.

"Champ," he gasped. "When baling hay, you need to drive forward by looking backward."

"Huh?"

"Watch the windrow, son. The outside row. The one exposed to the wind. If you keep the windrow shooting right up the middle of the baler mouth, everything else will fall into line. That way, you also keep your eye on the wagon and your pitiful passengers. We're feeling about as pitiful as pitiful gets."

"Backward is forward? Huh. Hey, why is Ray-Ray poking out of the baler?"

Next time, I would accept Uncle Rollie's offer to wear one of his ball caps. It would give me something to throw at the Basher. I wondered if I could carry rocks in it. I sure wasn't feeling sorry for him anymore.

"And for crying out loud, slow down. We're not on the road."

"Slow is dull."

"Son, faster will take longer because we'll have to stop every ten minutes to restack all the bales you bounce off the wagon. And to rebuild the baler after it shakes to pieces."

Bash shook his head. "Boring."

"Walking ain't crowded. Drive or walk. Your choice, buddy boy."

Uncle Rollie returned to the wagon. Bash slumped a little, then straightened up, shifted into a low gear, and eased out the clutch. The tractor barely jerked. I think snails raced past us. But at least our innards no longer threatened to become our outards. We ground along at a more reasonable *whhirrr-whhirrr, chunkaaa* up the side of the hayfield, turned where a fat creek cut through the farm to create twisty borders between fields, then puttered down the other side of the field along the woods until we turned again at the other end by the road.

Bash sat sideways in the tractor seat to watch the line of hay pass on his right and snake up the rotating spindles of the yellow baler mouth. The hay crammed through the baler, tied off into bales and bumped up the red chute, where

Uncle Rollie and I grabbed and stacked them like building blocks, higher and higher, into a sort of pyramid.

I yawned. "Not very exciting, is it?"

Uncle Rollie slung the next eighty-pound bale up to me where I sat seven rows up to shove it into place. "Work usually isn't. But it feels good." He scratched his bald spot. "And look, we're outside with machinery, stretching our muscles in the sunshine. I'm as happy as a hog in slop."

Chaff and bits of hay stuck to the sweat rolling down our arms and faces. I sniffed a mixture of freshly mown grass, axle grease, and tractor fumes, plus a bit of that hog slop stuff drifting over from the barns. And hay dust. "Ah-choo!" *Not very exciting at all.*

Then the rabbit showed up.

Chapter 10

A Baleful of Trouble

The brown bunny burst from its hiding place in the wind-row a few yards ahead of us and dashed toward the woods. Tractor Driver Bash popped out of his seat, turning to watch the rabbit run. Since he still held the steering wheel, the tractor started drifting across the field.

"*Hey!*" Uncle Rollie yelled.

Tractor Driver Bash whipped around to look at us, cutting the tractor even further into the field. The nearly nine-foot-tall stack of hay bales jostled, opening like an earthquake, then whomped back together. Add the four-foot height of the wagon, and I swayed thirteen dizzying feet off the ground while my nutso cousin played whip-the-wagon.

Bash jerked right and accidentally bumped the gas lever forward at about the same time a wagon wheel thunked into a rut. It didn't help at all that we were on a bit of slope. The wagon wobbled and shuddered, and another gap opened up between bales.

I threw myself lengthwise across the closest bale, snatching twine with each hand.

"Get me down from here. I mean, *keep me up here*. Don't fall, hay. Don't fall."

For a second, everything seemed fine. I wasn't sure if my bale still was sitting atop the rest of the stack or hovering above it.

Bash noticed my dilemma. "I got it."

He whipped the Allis-Chalmers back in line, but hadn't yet knocked the throttle back down to slow speed. The wagon thunked back over the rut, and with all the twisting and turning, tilted briefly onto two wheels before slamming back to all fours.

Half the load of hay stayed with the wagon. I was on the half that didn't.

"Learn to fly, learn to fly, *learn to fly!*" I warbled from atop my hay bale momentarily suspended thirteen feet in the air. Then I was riding the bale like a surfboard, skimming across a sweet-smelling, dry green wave of hay bales. I hoped my pants didn't flap off in the wind. Why hadn't I asked Uncle Rollie to punch more holes in my belt when I first noticed my jeans getting floppier?

As I recall, I yelled, "Cowabunga, dude!" Bash claims it sounded more like, *"Mommeeeeeeeeeeeee!"*

Bang. Bump. Boom. Oof. Pow. I ricocheted around a bit, bouncing off other bales, before hitting the ground with a thud. The breath exploded out of me. I still clutched my bale as it skidded another fifteen feet across the bumpy field like a snow sled at the bottom of a steep hill.

The ride finally stopped. My jeans stayed on—and mostly stayed up. My tight fingers still clutched the bale.

"Raymond!" Uncle Rollie's voice came from somewhere. "Raymond. *Ray.* Take a breath, boy."

Another, more annoying voice, broke in. "Ray-Ray Sunbeam Beamer, that was *Awe. Some.*"

Slowly I turned. And sucked in air. I was alive. Bash hadn't killed me. Oh, but I had some ideas for him. If only someone would pry my fingers from this baling twine burned into them and place them around his scrawny little . . .

Bash zipped around my hay bale. "My turn next!"

"Nicholas. Hush."

When your dad goes straight for your middle name, skipping right past the first, you know it's serious. Bash stopped yammering.

Uncle Rollie pried at my grip. "Ray, let go of the hay bale. Straighten this finger . . . now that one . . . and the next . . . Let's stand up . . . Whoa. Easy, feller."

I wobbled. My stomach lurched. My ears rang with what sounded like a tractor engine.

"The tractor." Uncle Rollie barely let loose of my elbow as

he swung around. "It's still moving. Didn't you stop it before jumping off?"

"Oops."

They both lit out after the tractor as it chugged across the field, the baler sucking up sections of hay as it cut across windrows and bore down on the creek. Another bale of hay plopped off out of the baler and onto the wagon just as the front wheels of the Allis sank into the creek.

That evening, the three of us perched on the edge of the empty wagon, chewing on strands of hay after storing the last of that day's baling in the haymow. We hadn't baled as much as Uncle Rollie meant for us to. After he towed the tractor out of the creek, we had to restack the toppled load of hay.

That's when he told Bash to crank the engine and finish baling, even though he tried to kill me and drown the tractor. Unreal! Now, we watched the sun fade into the far tree line. Uncle Rollie scratched his belly. "So . . . you two rode cows all the way to Clarey's?"

Please. It's been two weeks, almost three since that horrible day. Don't bring it up again! But Bash, of course, was eager. "Yep. Coulda made it all the way back, too, if Ma hadn't interrupted."

"Your Uncle Frankenstein, uh, Uncle Frank and I barely made it past the old Tillett place on our way to the corner store before your grandpa caught up to us."

My Dad? Did *what*?

Bash's eyes bulged. "Wow. That's so cool!"

Uncle Rollie stretched and yawned. A button nearly popped off the belly of his shirt. "Son."

"Yeah, Pops?"

"Don't do it again. Ever."

"Nope."

"Pretty good gag, though."

"Yeah!"

We all sat there, chewing the sweetness off the ends of our pieces of hay. Something still bugged me. Sure, the rest of the day had crawled by with no more wild hayrides, no more rabbits, and no more tractor hops. But why did Uncle Rollie risk it? Finally, I exploded: "Why'd you let Bash near a tractor again?"

Uncle Rollie took a swig from the water jug and wiped his mouth on his sleeve. "To tell the truth, I wanted to get your Aunt Matilda to drive the tractor and send Bash to the house to babysit his sister."

"Hey," Bash yelped.

"But the boy's got to learn sometime. I figure if God can be as patient a Father as He is with me, I ought to try the same with my own son."

Why would God waste His time on tractors? Or Bash? He sure didn't waste much time on me. Uncle Rollie scrunched the top of Bash's ball cap. "I reckon it wasn't God's fault the way I turned out. The Basher here . . . well, I suppose there is something to heredity."

"Whatcha mean, Pops?"

"The first time your grandpa let me bale, the tractor tried to climb a tree. Gramps about had a conniption fit. Then he put me back on the tractor. I learned how to bale and about a father's patience for knucklehead sons."

Bash chewed his tongue. "But I'm not . . . well, maybe sometimes."

Patience? I'd been too patient. I nearly felt sorry for the Basher today. He ruined that. I'd bean Bash the first chance I got. Patience. Yeah, I'd get him.

Uncle Rollie slid off the wagon. He rubbed his brightening bald spot and looked around. "Has anyone seen my hat?"

Uh-oh.

Chatper 11

Basher and Goliath

A new Sunday school teacher stepped in almost every week at Laughing Brook Bible Church. Miss Caldwell, the latest volunteer, apparently thought she'd figured out a way to hold our interest: "Starting next week, you will be teaching the lessons to each other. Won't that be fun?"

Kenny Matthews's hand shot up. "Ooh, Marty should teach about Noah and the flood. He forgot to turn off the faucet in the boys' room last week."

Marty leaped out of his chair, which collapsed in a folded wooden heap. "Did not! I saw Chet go in after me."

Kenny smirked. "Maybe it wasn't the faucet, either."

Chet Rodgers gulped down a bite of candy from the bar hidden in his pocket. "Not me. I wasn't here last week. I had the measles pox. I might still have some. I bet if I touch Sarah on the arm, she'll break out in red polka dots just as big as the ones on Jag's dress."

"Get away from me!" Sarah Tisdale jumped so hard, she knocked Mary Jane Morris right off her chair, and they both landed in a heap of frills and curls. It was the funniest thing that we boys had seen in at least thirty seconds and we howled. The girls dove around Sarah and Mary Jane, dusting them off. From somewhere inside the pile came Sarah's voice: "It's not *measles* pox, it's chickenpox."

Miss Caldwell lost her smile. "Class. *Class!* Come. To. Order!"

Something clump-clump-clumped on the other side of the wall. Old Mr. Hopkins beating on the cement block wall with his crooked stick cane. We burst out laughing again.

Miss Caldwell clapped her hands like one big gunshot. "*That's. It.* Now sit down, hush up, and put on your listening ears."

Listening ears? Marty flicked his finger through his mouth to make popping noises as Kenny pretended to pluck off his ears. "Look, I'm Mr. Potato Head. Does anybody need some listening ears? I'm not using mine."

We nearly busted a gut again but it looked like we'd pushed Miss Caldwell about as far as was safe. Kenny snapped his pretend ears back into place. We punched each other on the shoulders until we quieted each other down.

Miss Caldwell blew a strand of hair off her forehead and rubbed her temples. "Now, as I said, starting next week, you will take turns telling the Sunday school story using the flannel board. You will illustrate each part by placing these flannel cutouts of scenery and people on the board like so . . ."

From a folder, she plucked what looked like paper dolls snipped out of cloth. One colored-in cutout looked like a tree and the other, a guy in a bathrobe. She placed them on a fuzzy, cloth-covered board sitting on an easel and rubbed them into place. They stuck without glue or Velcro or anything that I could see.

Miss Caldwell peeled the bathrobe guy off the board. "When you get to the next part of your Bible story, you'll change the scenes. You'll be a talking book and these are your pictures."

Mary Jane sat up straight in her chair. "That sounds like a wonderful idea, Miss Caldwell."

She thought she was so mature just because she was twelve already and would be graduating to the teens' class soon. I looked down at her pointy-toed cowboy boots and decided to keep my mouth shut.

"How do we know which scenes to do when?" Mary Jane asked in her teacher's-pet voice.

"It's all diagrammed in the story booklet that I will give you a week before it's your turn. Then you can practice and tell the story in your own words."

Bash snickered. "If Mary Jane uses her own words, it'll take three Sundays to tell the story."

Miss Caldwell spun on her heel. "Sebastian, you have just

volunteered to be the first Sunday school teacher. Next week, you will tell us the story of David and Goliath. Here's the teacher's booklet. Use your Bible for research. The adventure of Goliath is chapter 17 of 1 Samuel."

Bash gaped at her with bug eyes. Then he caught a glimpse of Mary Jane's smirk. "Thank you, Miss Caldwell. This will be the best lesson ever. You'll see."

Miss Caldwell paled. I shuddered. Whenever Bash vowed to do his best, I knew I was in for the worst of it.

Back in his room after church, Bash spread the flannel-paper cutouts across his bed. He slid them this way and that, paused, shook his head, swept the cutouts back into a pile and started over again. It looked like trying to put together a puzzle from pieces spilled from three boxes.

Bash frowned over the paper dollies like he expected them to talk. He scratched his ear. "God might be calling me to be a preacher. I better find out."

All that week, Preacher Bash locked me out of our room for a couple hours a day so he could study the story of David and play with his flannel dollies instead of me.

"They're not dolls," he snapped through the closed door when I pounded on it Wednesday. "They're flannel teaching tools. All of us preachers use them to teach you little kids."

"It's a Sunday school lesson. And I'm still older than you. And taller."

"Fatter too. I guess Miss Caldwell knows maturity when she sees it."

My back to the door, I slid down until I thumped to the floor. I heard Bash slide down his side of the door. He mumbled like he was reading something. I heard rustling noises, maybe like flannel dollies swishing across the floor. More mumbling. More swishing. For weeks, I wished he'd just leave me alone and out of his crazy schemes. Now that he did, I couldn't stand it.

"C'mon, Bash, tell me what you're going to do."

"Nope. It's a surprise. But it'll be good."

"Does your mom know?"

"That's why I can't tell you. You'll blab."

"Will not. And why won't you tell your mom?"

"It'll ruin the surprise."

I heard him clambering about. I scrambled to my feet just as the bedroom door whipped open. Bash bounded out with a giant green and yellow backpack in hand. "Stay here. I gotta go see if the supplies will fit."

"What supplies? Miss Caldwell gave you everything."

Bash stuck out his chest. "For a regular, boring lesson, sure. But we're going to have the best lesson ever with visual aids way better than flannel doll . . . I mean, flannel teaching tools."

"Let me help." *I can't believe I just said that.*

"No. You stay here."

"Please." *Idiot!*

Bash scratched his head with the backpack. It looked big enough to carry a tent. Or to be the tent. "Tell you what.

Round up some old tin cans. I need 'em for the lesson. And find Pops's old work boots, the ones he hardly ever uses anymore. And I promise, Sunday morning, I'll let you help with the lesson.

"Oh, and tell Ma I had to run to Bonkers's house to pick up visual aids for the lesson."

What visual aids? Bonkers had cats, dogs, gerbils, snakes, rabbits, birds, mice, toads, and I don't know what else. I knew enough about Bible stories to know that nothing at Bonkers's place had anything to do with a giant warrior like Goliath.

Fine! If twerpy-twerp Bash wanted to play with Bonkers's kittens instead of letting me help him with his flannel dollies, let him. Big deal.

I stomped outside after him. While Bash darted toward the woods, I rooted through trash and recycling containers behind the house for tomato soup cans or whatever might be handy. But I wasn't rinsing them out. If he wouldn't tell me his secrets, Bash could wash out his own tin cans.

Sunday morning finally came. Just before we left for church, the Basher darted to the barn and came back clutching the giant backpack with both hands. He stashed it in the trunk of the family car and wouldn't talk about it.

Aunt Tillie's eye ticked a flap or two. "Bash, please tell me that you aren't smuggling your water cannon to church again."

"Nah, I'm teaching about David and Goliath, not the Battle of Jericho. Besides, I was a little kid then. I thought they used cannons in the Bible." Bash shrugged. "But I got the other part right. When Mrs. Ledder got to the part about blowing the trumpets and shouting, she was so busy puttin' stuff on the flannel board that she never saw us whip out our horns and kazoos. She tried to knock the wall down by herself when we blew our horns. We didn't know she'd play along so well."

Uncle Rollie rubbed his chin. "You know, it's been eight months and Elsie Ledder still hasn't returned to church."

Aunt Tillie shook her head. "She listens to services on the radio now. She says she feels safer having church where she can triple lock the door."

Bash's eyes fairly glittered with the same horrible sparkle I saw just before I tried tipping over a cow. The same sparkle I saw when he taunted me into riding a cow. And just before I surfed a hay bale off a loaded wagon.

My stomach lurched. I bet that the radio preacher was about to have a lot more business.

Chapter 12

The Slingshot and David's Zoo

Even Bash's giant backpack seemed to quiver with excitement in Sunday school as he stowed it between his seat and the wall.

"What's the Basher gonna do?" Jig Gobnotter whispered. Jig wore one of his Sunday baseball caps, a red one with "Jesus Saves" printed on it in yellow.

"It's a surprise."

"Wouldn't tell you, either, huh?"

Miss Caldwell peeked into the room before tiptoeing inside. "You know, Sebastian, perhaps I rushed you into this assignment. It would be fine with me if you'd rather not . . ."

Preacher Bash leaped to his feet. "Nope, I'm ready."

"It's just that, well . . . are you sure?"

"Let's go." Preacher Basher dragged the backpack to the flannel board. He hunched over the bag. We heard the zipper. Bash rummaged around a bit. "Shh!" *Seven seconds as a teacher and he's shushing us already?*

Preacher Bash straightened and faced us, clutching the folder of flannel board cutouts. "Today, brothers and sisters, we are going to learn about David and Goliath."

Mary Jane shook her chocolate brown curls and scrunched up her nose. "If Sebastian Nicholas Hinglehobb was my brother . . ."

"We're all brothers and sisters in the Lord when we believe!" Bash boomed in his best preacher voice. "But today, we need to talk about a farmer boy named David."

Bash snatched a piece of yellowish flannel from the folder and rubbed it across the bottom of the blue felt board. Next, Bash smoothed purplish mountains into place, then added trees, tufts of grass and a big rock. Onto the rock, he placed a cutout of a sitting boy wearing brown sandals, a yellow bed sheet and holding a big stick. "This is David. He's a sheep farmer."

Sarah huffed. "It's called 'shepherd.'"

Bash positioned cutouts of sheep around David. "David watched all of his dad Jess's sheep."

Sarah the Corrector corrected: "Jess-SEE. The name is Jesse."

Bash ignored her. "David was the little brother out of eight boys so he got stuck doing all the yucky jobs. Lesson number one—try not to be born last."

"You can't . . . *Ooooohh!*" Sarah's knuckles turned white where she gripped the sides of her seat like she was trying to keep herself from exploding.

Bash swept David, the sheep and the trees off the flannel board, then placed tiny groups of tents and men in the background on either side of the board. In the middle, he plunked a warrior, much bigger than the David cutout. The warrior wore mostly armor. Armor lapped over his shins. Armor plates hung from his shoulders and covered his upper body. Black hair and a bushy beard gushed from beneath an armored helmet.

"This is Goliath, a warrior."

We boys leaned forward. A shield covered most of one giant arm. With his other big hand, the giant clutched a long, thick sword.

Bash tapped the sword. "He carried the world's biggest spear." Sarah didn't correct him.

"He also carried the world's biggest javelin." A smaller sword handle poked up behind Goliath where it strapped onto his back.

"Goliath the warrior towered nine feet, nine inches tall. He could dunk a basketball sitting down. Only he woulda popped the ball like a balloon 'cause he was strong and mean."

Miss Caldwell started to say something but clamped her mouth shut. Bash kept preaching. "So while Farmer David got stuck staying home doing chores, his brothers got to go off to war and have fun."

Sarah sighed. "Shepherd boy."

"One day, David's dad, Jess—Jess-SEE, I mean—sent him to take food to his brothers. And that's when David saw big ol' Goliath teasing the soldiers. Goliath yelled across the valley, 'Na-na-na-na-naaa, you can't beat me. Fraidy-cat sissies. C'mon, you bock-bock-bock chickens. Send out your best guy, and if he beats me, our army will surrender.' It probably was a trick but it didn't matter. The soldiers really *were* afraid."

We boys booed the cowards and booed the showoff giant. Bash joined in. We booed so loudly that I thought I saw Bash's green and yellow backpack tremble. Miss Caldwell jammed a finger to her lips. When we heard Mr. Hopkins's cane whap against the wall, Preacher Bash raised his hands. We hushed to hear what came next.

"While the grown-ups shook in fear, Farmer Boy David knew what to do."

We boys cheered. Jag Gobnotter snorted. Sarah Tisdale rolled her eyes.

"Farmer David knew that God's bigger'n any giant."

Bash stooped over his backpack a second then spun to face me. "Brother Beamer, this is the part where you get to help. Put this tin can on your head and stand over there by the wall like that."

Bash dug into the backpack. "Shh," he said, even though

we weren't talking much. He yanked out his Indiana Jones adventurer's pouch and slung it over his shoulder.

"David ran out to meet Goliath. Instead of spears and javelins, David had his farmer's kit—"

Sarah huffed. "Shepherd's pouch."

"—and a slingshot." From the pouch, Bash pulled a slingshot built from rawhide bootlaces strung through the leather tongue of old work boots. He pulled a smooth creek stone from the pouch, loaded the slingshot, and started twirling the thing over his head.

Across the room, a bit of tomato soup dribbled down my hair. Maybe I should have cleaned the cans. Suddenly, I figured out what "helping" meant.

"Basher. Wait!"

Too late. Bash let go of one end of the bootlace. One shiny creek stone whipped across the room . . . and knocked over a stack of hymnals in the far corner.

Jig snickered.

Bash slapped the air. "Nuts. Hold on, Beamer, I can do this. I practiced in the woods. Besides, remember the lesson—when God guides the stone, it goes exactly where it needs to be."

Mary Jane scrambled under her chair, her pointy-toed cowboy points sticking out. "Well, give God the slingshot, then. Your aim stinks!"

Another stone whizzed through the air and ricocheted off the block walls two or three times before landing in Jag's flower-printed lap. Jag somersaulted into the air like she'd been shot and the stone flew from her lap and clunked Chet Rodgers in the back. "Ow. Watch it."

Miss Caldwell swatted a third stone out of the air with her Bible. "Sebastian! Stop that this instant!"

Bash loaded a fourth stone. "It's okay, Miss C. I've got it now."

I froze. By now I knew the safest place to stand was wherever Bash aimed. The pebble plinked the wastebasket. Bash's aim did stink.

I remembered from the song "Only a Boy Named David" that David took five stones from the babbling brook. Bash should just about be out of ammo.

A couple of the girls screamed and tried to huddle underneath the folding chairs with Mary Jane. Billy Loomis asked if he could try the slingshot next. Bash whipped his last shot. The water glass Miss Caldwell kept shattered, soaking a stack of Sunday school papers. "Oops."

Bash stuffed the slingshot into his pouch. He rumbled out with his preacher voice again. "When King Saul asked David why he dared go after Goliath, David told him because he practiced as a farm boy. He killed both a lion and a bear when they attacked his sheep. God let him beat all the bad guys."

Mary Jane crawled from beneath her chair. "That's not how the story goes."

"It is!" Preacher Bash thundered, waving his arms. "I'll show you how it works." He leaned over his backpack again. "I couldn't capture any lions or bears in the woods to demonstrate this part, so . . ."

Bash pulled out a small cage. One of Bonkers's mourning doves flapped and cooed. "Pretend this is our lion."

I couldn't tell whether the cooing lion was Bonkers's dove Marge or his dove Hannah because once Basher opened the cage, she flapped around the room in a flurry.

"And these mice are our sheep." Preacher Bash opened a box he pulled from the backpack.

A dozen or so brown and white mice streaked across the room. One ran right up Miss Caldwell's leg and held on tight as Miss Caldwell hopped and screamed. She tried to dig footholds into the cement blocks of the wall. She finally let go and fell when Hannah—or possibly Marge—swooped into her hair for a rest.

That's when a black face with a pointy nose poked out of the bag. Furry white head, black rounded ears and a streak of white running from its forehead to the tip of his blackish nose.

Skunk!

"And here's our bear!" Preacher Bash shouted over the tumult.

Buster, Bonkers's pet skunk, never wanted to miss out on the action. He swept one black foreleg out of the backpack, then the other, tipping over the bag as he shook it from his hind legs and waddled out. Pleased with himself, he flashed his bushy tail in the air and stretched, giving us a good view of where the white streak on his head and neck separated into two white stripes along either side of his broad back.

Miss Caldwell flung open the classroom door and hurtled out just as a bunch of the guys from the men's Sunday school class across the hall rushed over. She slammed headfirst into Mr. Whitney's stomach. Big ol' Mr. Whitney looked more like a bear than Buster did. Miss Caldwell dropped him just like a little stone knocking down a giant.

Three other men sidestepped them. But just as they reached the doorway, Mr. Collins bellowed, "Wha . . . *Skunk!*"

"Aaarghh! A mouse! *Another one!*" Herbie Peterson from the teens' class. He ran into the nursery and we heard what sounded like somebody jumping into one of the cribs.

Jag snorted. "Just like a boy."

Another grown-up peeked into the classroom. *"Skunk! Skunk!"* He turned and vaulted over pews and a couple of the ladies.

"Somebody call the fire department!"

The few of us kids who didn't run from the skunk roared with laughter. We'd never seen such a movement of the spirit in church.

"Hi, Buster." Mary Jane cooed as she scooped the skunk into her arms. He fairly purred, if skunks could purr, as he nuzzled into Mary Jane's chocolate curls, his white-striped tail swishing back and forth. Buster would cuddle with anyone, even Mary Jane.

Mary Jane held Buster out to Sarah. "It's okay, Sarah. He's de-scented. He's one of Christopher Joseph Dennison's pets. They've got a skunk license."

Bash glowered at the panicking adults. "They're fraidy-cats just like Israel's army facing Goliath. Well, we better rescue the mice before they get stomped on. Beamer, take the tin can off your head and use it to carry them back to their box"

"There's still some soup in here."

"That's okay. They probably need some to calm their nerves." I picked up a brown mouse nibbling on soaked Sunday school papers. "So how come you didn't bring sheep to be the sheep?"

"They wouldn't fit in the bag."

"Oh."

Our new Sunday school teacher, old Mr. Hopkins, promised to never let any of us teach a class again. He thumped his crooked cane on the floor if he thought we were breathing too loudly.

That afternoon, Bash and I sprawled in his room, wondering how many years we'd be grounded.

Bash tossed a basketball at the ceiling. "Did you get all of Bonkers's mice scooped up?"

"All but two. Freckles and Junior decided to become church mice."

Bash spun the ball in his hands, then tossed it again. "Did you tell anyone?"

"I thought it best not to mention it."

Bash tucked the ball under his head. "Probably right. You know, Beamer, I don't think God's calling me into the ministry."

"Well, duh!"

"I sure tried. I even had more lessons planned."

I rolled onto my side and stared at him. "Like what?"

"Remember the story when Jesus let the demons infest the herd of pigs? That would be a great one for visual aids. I could train my riding pig Gulliver J. McFrederick the Third to lead the charge of all our hogs right down the center aisle and they could leap into the baptismal tub."

I flopped onto my pillow and squeezed my eyes shut. It was hard to get rid of that picture.

Bash sat up. "And don't forget the dancing bones in Ezekiel. I already collected my visual aids. I stored them under your bed. You were going to be my assistant preacher."

"Um . . ." I wanted to know what visual aids lurked beneath my bed. Rotting raccoons? Molted lizard skins? That rabbit skull he found in the woods a few weeks back?

I didn't ask. Instead, I pulled Bash's slingshot closer to where I could snatch it up in a hurry. Just in case.

Could anything worse happen before this nightmare ended?

Stupid question.

Chapter 13

The Pirate Fleet

Two mornings later, I stepped carefully toward the house while hugging a basket heaped with twenty-four brown, pink, and white eggs we'd collected from the chicken coop. Twenty-four eggs, one more than yesterday morning's haul, grow heavy in a hurry when you're trying not to trip over things like driveway rocks, loose shoelaces, or babbling cousins running circles around you.

Bash snagged a dirty brown egg from the basket, tossed it in the air and caught it. "I would have made a great pirate captain."

I hated it when Bash blurted out something because it usually meant I'd soon be dressed in bandages, antiseptic, poison ivy cream, ice packs, tetanus shots, crutches, or possibly a tombstone.

I stopped—carefully. "Put that egg back. Your mom told me no cracked ones today."

Bash set the egg on top of the heap. It rolled down the egg hill and clunked against the side of the basket. It didn't break. I hugged the basket more tightly and let out my breath. "Stop playing with your food."

I hated collecting the eggs every morning and evening. The chickens pecked my toes, their feathers made my eyes water, and Aunt Tillie expected me to get all the eggs into the house without Bash breaking any.

"Maybe you ought to give preaching another whirl." At least preaching would be indoors. I'd caught a bit of a summer cold from wandering in the woods at night and getting drenched in the storm, and I'd finally stopped sneezing. This summer couldn't end fast enough so I could escape this asylum.

Bash shook his straw-colored head. "Nope. We're pirates now."

Bash held open the back door. I climbed the porch steps, tapping my feet twice on each stair before taking the next step. A guy needs to be careful with eggs—and chicken-brained cousins. "You are not sawing off my leg so that I can have a peg leg."

Bash grinned and started filling the sink. "Still won't do that? It would be fun. Everybody would want to see it."

"Then why don't you have the pirate peg leg?"

I gently placed eggs in the water one at a time and washed straw and crud off the shells. Chickens are messy. Bash picked up each clean egg, dried it, and filled cartons from the stack. "Nah, I'm the only one who can saw straight."

"Really? Let me try."

"Let's just wear the eye patches again."

I thought so. I closed the filled cartons and carried them one at a time to the produce cooler. Aunt Tillie had plenty of customers among the neighbors for her eggs.

Bash dried his hands. "But this time we need a real pirate ship. And a real crew."

"Where are we going to get those? Pirates Arrr Us?"

"Hey, I've got an idea!" Bash zoomed out the door so fast that the glow in his eyes left light tracks, like contrails after a fighter jet.

I considered pausing long enough to tell Aunt Tillie to round up the bandages, antiseptic, poison ivy cream, ice packs, tetanus shots, crutches, and possibly a tombstone, but I hadn't seen her eye tic all day and I didn't want it to start up again now. Maybe I could get her to wear Bash's eye patch.

I plucked the last egg out of the sink. Bash must have missed it. I headed to the cooler, tossing the egg in the air, and wondering what disaster my crazy cousin planned now.

I missed the egg. *Splat.* Egg guts exploded across the floor. When did I start playing catch with food? Well, I knew where the rags and broom were—right where we left them after yesterday's mess. I sighed and cleaned up.

Five minutes later, I trailed after the Basher across the hayfield and into the orchard, where he perched atop Look Out Fort, our apple treetop hideaway at the edge of the jungle.

"That's why this tree fort was so crummy." Bash stomped on the old, blue shed door that we used as a floor for Look Out Fort. "It's because it's not a fort."

"Told you. Anybody can see it's a stupid door from a stupid falling down shed, and it's not a stupid tree fort."

"Don't be stupid, Ray-Ray Sunbeam Beamer. Of course it's not a fort. It's a boat. I should have recognized it right off."

"Stop calling me that. And it still looks like a door to me. See, the doorknob's even on it."

Bash wasn't listening to me. "Let's get some hammers and pry the walls and benches and everything else off of here. We've got a pirate ship to build."

"Aren't pirates evil? I thought you were too much of a goodie-goodie barn boots to be a pirate."

Pirate Captain Bash stuck his nose in the air, thrust out his chest and folded one arm behind his back in a pirate captain pose. "I'm the nice kind of pirate. I stop ships on the high seas and give them presents. I'm like Santa Pirate."

I kicked at the plywood fort wall and watched it wobble. "Where do you get the presents?"

"God gives 'em. Remember our memory verse from Sunday? Something like if you, being bad people, know how to give good gifts, how many more presents will your Father in heaven give to those who ask Him? (see Matt. 7:11). See? We're God's pirate delivery service."

I rolled my eyes. "I remember the verse a few weeks ago. It said that if any of you lacks brains, ask God and God will give them to him. James-something. Try that verse on for size."

"Beamer, you think too much. God gives good gifts."

"Not thinking gives a guy broken bones."

I peered back at the house. If we went inside, Aunt Tillie probably would send us to muck the pig hutches or something. I stomped on the door floor. I supposed there were worse things to do than to turn our tree fort into a pirate ship. It wasn't much of a tree fort. I mean, there was a doorknob sticking out of the floor. I sighed. "So who's our crew?"

Pirate Captain Bash brightened. "Gulliver J. McFrederick the Third will be first mate."

"Your riding hog is a sailing hog too?"

Bash paced circles around me. "And I think we'll build a flotilla of other ships from bottles and boxes, and see if Bonkers has some mice to captain the other boats."

"And me?"

Bash planted himself in front of me, his timbers practically shivering with excitement. "You can be first swab. C'mon, it'll be fun."

"Wait. I rank below the pig?"

"Oh." Bash tugged on an imaginary pirate beard for a moment. "Hey, I know, Gulliver J. McFrederick the Third will be the pirate captain. I'll be second mate and admiral. You'll be chief assistant swab!"

"Chief. That's better. Chief is best. Gimme the other hammer."

We kicked down the fort walls and tossed to the ground the stools and the bunk we'd started. I dug at nails with the hammer claw, popping them out bent and crooked. I jammed the old nails into my pants pockets and discovered I wore the same jeans I had on when we built the fort. The nails finished off the parts of the pockets not already shredded. Bent nails tumbled down my legs, digging fresh scratches into my skin before scattering at my feet.

I handed the bent nails to Bash. "Here, put these in your pocket."

"No way. Only a dummy would carry nails in his pocket."

"But you were the one who told me to do that when we built the fort."

"Yep."

"Hey."

"I mean, Chief Assistant Swab Dummy."

"Pirate Captain Possum-Face."

Bash laughed so hard he almost fell out of the remains of Look Out Fort. I tried to help him but he jumped out of the way.

I wondered if I needed bandages, antiseptic, or tetanus shots for the nail scratches, and maybe a rabies shot to protect me from Bash.

Pretty soon, we had our tree fort disassembled. We carted the heavy ol' blue door floor to the duck pond way out past the pigpen with all its hutches for the hogs. With the mid-July sun, sweat rolled down our faces and stuck our shirts to our backs. We stopped a couple times to huff and puff before finally packing that door in.

The pond—or possibly small lake—stretched a long way. The ducks could invite every duck, goose, egret and sea gull I'd ever seen in my life to a party and there'd still be room for three hippos and a sea monster. A couple of fishing piers perched along the banks. Cattails grew around the shallower edges, lily pads, and other floating gunk bobbed further out, and lots and lots of clear water glistened in the middle.

Whoever dug the pond built it just below the creek that meandered through Uncle Rollie's farm. The admiral pointed to where the creek touched the top of the pond in a couple places.

"If we sail out the pond and into Conneaut Creek, our pirate ship would flow all the way to Lake Erie. We'd bob helplessly up the St. Lawrence Seaway, shoot over Niagara Falls, drift through locks and canals and pop out into the Atlantic Ocean where we'd be lost forever. It would be so cool."

It amazed me that Uncle Rollie kept such a dangerous pond.

We began searching for shipbuilding materials. We found fence posts stacked in a heap at the back of the tractor barn.

I hefted one of the posts. "Won't your dad need these?"

Bash curled a post beneath each arm. "He's not gonna build the new fence until fall. He won't care if we use a few now if we give 'em back before then."

I scooped up a second post. "What if he does?"

"Stop worrying. You'll get warts. We didn't get in trouble for building Look Out Fort, did we?"

"Not yet."

Bash shifted the posts so the back ends dragged on the ground. He looked ready to pull a pony cart without the cart. Or the pony. "See."

"But your mom—"

"C'mon, these posts get heavier the longer we hold 'em." Bash took off, the two fence poles clunking behind him.

I hefted the posts in my arms. How did I keep getting into these things? I sighed and clunked after Bash.

It took a few trips to collect enough poles to support the blue door floor of the pirate ship. Bash whacked a gob of baling twine out of the baler so we could tie the posts together like a raft.

A voice interrupted as we lashed posts together: "Whatcha doin'?"

"Oh, hey, Bonkers." Uncle Jake O'Rusty Whatever trotted alongside Bonk, his tongue wagging. The dog's tongue, I mean, not Bonkers's.

"We're building a flotilla of pirate ships."

I strained at a knot. "But we've only got one shed door, so we only can make one ship. Aunt Tillie would notice if we took the house doors."

The admiral jumped up. "This will be the flagship. Gulliver J. McFrederick the Third's gonna sail it. He's the captain."

I stopped tying. "Nuh-uh. Gulliver's first mate. I'm chief."

"Keep tying those knots, Chief Assistant Swab." Bash turned back to Bonkers. "We're going to build a bunch of smaller ships out of shoeboxes and plastic bottles and stuff. Wanna round up some of your critters for a crew?"

"How about my rabbits, Goo-Goo, Gee-Gee, and Ga-Ga?"

My baling twine knot slipped. "Goo-Goo, Gee-Gee, and Ga-Ga? What kind of names are those?"

Bonkers shrugged. "Darla named them. I wanted to call them Brutus, Braveheart, and Bingo."

I slapped the door. Deck, I mean. "They're rabbits. You can't put rabbits on pirate ships no matter what you call them. They don't swim."

Bonkers rolled a fence post toward the raft and grabbed some twine. "Of course rabbits swim. They're real good swimmers. I can hardly keep Goo-Goo, Gee-Gee, and Ga-Ga out of the swimming pool."

I fumbled with a knot. "You take your pets swimming?"

"Not a pool like you city kids have. Chlorine's bad for them. We have a little pool just for the pets. It's how I give them baths."

Weirdos. Bonkers reached for another fence post and a hunk of twine. "Don't you have animals that swim where you come from?"

"Yeah. They're called dolphins. And jellyfish, loggerhead turtles, and sharks. They're supposed to be in the water. Not rabbits and mice."

"Mice swim too." Bonkers twisted twine around a pole. "Raccoons are the best. And snakes. Hedgehogs love swimming but they stink at it. I'm not bringing Ralphie the hedgehog. In case there's a goof."

I choked. "In case there's a goof? Has anything you guys did ever *not* gone wrong?"

Second Mate and Pirate Admiral Bash grinned. "That's the stuff that's the most fun, Beamer." He threw a salute at Bonkers. "Welcome aboard, Recruitment Officer Bonkers. We've got a crew."

We snugged the posts together as tightly as we could, running the baling twine around each post. Bash concentrated so hard on cinching posts that I thought he'd gnaw off his tongue. Maybe it would be safer if he wagged his tongue like Uncle Jake.

We found leftover chunks of boards in Uncle Rollie's shop, scooped up some straight nails—which I carried in an old tin can this time around—and hammered the boards to the door and poles to hold them together.

We heard voices above our huffing and puffing. Jig and Jag rounded the path to the dock. Today, Jig wore an *Edna's House of Flies and Worms and Beauty Salon* cap and Jag's yellow dress with green daisies didn't quite cover the legs of the baggy, purple gym shorts flapping below her knees. Jig spotted our raft and ran to run a hand along the bow. Or possibly the aft. "Wow. This is great. Awesome." He scratched his hat. "What is it?"

Jag crossed her arms and eyes. "Whatever it is, it probably won't float."

Recruitment Officer Bonkers wiped his brow. "We're building a pirate fleet. My mice and rabbits are going to crew some smaller ships. And maybe Ralph the raccoon."

I poked my glasses up my nose. "I thought Ralph was your hedgehog."

"Nope. Ralphie's the hedgehog. Just plain Ralph's the raccoon. And Ralpher's my ferret, Ray."

"Ridiculous."

Bonkers pointed a nail at the raft. "And Bash's riding pig is going to captain the flagship."

Jig's eyes grew wide and his cap bobbed. "Cool. Jag, let's get that bucket over there and hire some frogs and turtles out of the cattails. More pirates for the ships."

Jag scanned the empty pond and snorted. "What ships?"

Bash used his hammer to reach an itch between his shoulder blades. "We're gonna build 'em. From wooden stools, plastic boxes, and fruit bowls and stuff."

"Sebastian Nicholas Hinglehobb, that's crazy." Bash's pesky neighbor Mary Jane Morris glided her bicycle to a stop. Farm kids must turn out by the herd to take part in a good disaster.

"Hi, MJ." Jag didn't snort.

"Hello, Jecolia." Mary Jane didn't sneer.

She eyed the rest of us, checking off our full names on her fingers as if taking inventory at Morris's Corner Store and Seed Emporium, though not as pleasantly: "Jehoshaphat Isaac Gobnotter. Christopher Joseph Dennison. Raymond William Boxby."

Uncle Jake slurped the back of Mary Jane's hand, then ran off to chase ducks.

Mary Jane ticked off a finger. "Dumb dog." She wiped dog slobber onto Jig's shirt. "What are you little kids up to?"

Sailor Jig jumped up, empty bucket swinging from his hand. "We're building a pirate fleet."

Second Mate and Pirate Admiral Bash patted the aft, or possibly the bow, of the raft. "This will be the flagship."

Maybe Mary Jane could stop this lunacy. I waved at Bash. "He thinks his stupid pig will sail it into the pond." I shook another finger at Bonkers. "And he thinks rabbits swim."

Mary Jane rolled her eyes. "Of course rabbits can swim. My bunnies would rather hop, but Christopher's rabbits love swimming."

Recruitment Officer Bonkers nodded so hard his cap almost fell off. "Yeah. My mice and bunnies are going to command the rest of the pirate flotilla. And maybe some of my snakes. We're gonna use old shoes and Tupperware dishes and anything else that floats to make boats."

Cannon Marksman Jag took the pail from Sailor Jig. "We're gonna catch turtles and frogs for more sailors."

Mary Jane smirked her superior twelve-year-old smirk. "Another half-witted idea brought to you by half-wits."

Sailor Jig shook his head. "If Bash is a half-wit and Ray is a half-wit, that equals one full wit. So it's a full-witted idea. It'll work."

Jag and Mary Jane rolled their eyes at the same time.

It was my turn to speak up. "It wasn't my idea."

The admiral took no notice. "Okay, pirates, let's go get the rest of the flotilla. We set sail after lunch."

Aunt Tillie slid sloppy joes onto our plates next to freshly picked green beans. Too bad the Hinglehobbs hadn't planted potato chip bushes instead.

She handed Bash his plate. "I saw all the kids over. What are you hoodlums up to today?"

"We're gonna sail pirate ships on the pond."

Uncle Rollie, in from the fields, winked at Bash. "Too bad your ma won't let me get a rowboat."

"It's because *your* son would sail the rowboat to the ocean."

"C'mon, Ma. Gulliver J. McFrederick the Third could steer."

Aunt Tillie's eyelid quivered. "No."

Bash sighed. "Guess we're stuck with the little boats on hand."

"So you're finally going to use those little, boat-shaped sponges that Aunt Rosie gave you for Christmas. Well, be careful."

"Oh, yeah. I forgot about the bath toys. Those'll be great with the ones we build. Thanks, Ma."

Aunt Tillie started to say something else but shook her head and walked away to massage her temple.

Uncle Rollie wiped sloppy joe dribble from his mouth. "Watch out for sharks."

"*What?*"

Bash grinned. "He's teasing."

"I knew that."

After lunch—or dinner, as they called it—Uncle Rollie headed back to the fields and Aunt Tillie went off to put

Darla down for her nap. We dashed through the house collecting the rest of the flotilla. Bash carefully emptied every cereal box onto the cabinet shelves, leaving neat piles of flakes and circles and squares. With a stack of Popsicle sticks from the toy box, he built fences around each pile so his mom wouldn't get angry. Then we threw the empty cereal boxes into a plastic garbage sack—our sailor's sea bag.

Bash slung a roll of plastic wrap into the bag. "We'll wrap this around the boxes that aren't plastic-coated. That'll keep 'em from sinking. Grab the wax paper and tin foil too."

We poured laundry soap and bleach out of their plastic bottles into rows of coffee mugs we stacked on top of the washer and dryer.

I tapped the bottom of a detergent bottle to get the rest of the blue soapy stuff out. "Are you sure this is okay, Bash? It doesn't seem like something your mom will like. Maybe we should ask."

Bash jammed a bleach bottle into our sea duffel bag. "Don't need to ask. You heard Ma. She said we could use little boats."

"She meant the boat sponges."

"She meant everything in the house we could use as a boat. She knows we need more than three sponges. I told her that."

"That's not exactly what you said. We better—"

"C'mon, Beams, there's more stuff in the kitchen we can use. Let's go."

"But—" But he was gone.

Well, it was his mom. He should know what's okay. We

weren't ruining anything. All the soap and cereal and stuff was still there where Aunt Tillie could use it. I poked my glasses back up my nose and headed for the kitchen.

We snagged a couple salad bowls that we hadn't seen Aunt Tillie use in at least a month. A plastic-coated shoe-box full of bills and papers sat on the desk. We jammed the papers into a bag we found in the trash, tossed the bag on the desk, and took the shoebox.

We collected hankies and cloth napkins for sails and wooden mixing spoons for oars. Our sea bag threatened to burst. Time to hit the high seas.

"Oops." Bash darted into the bathroom. "Almost forgot Aunt Rosie's sponge boats."

We dumped our pirated supplies at the pond, then ran to round up more. Bash said his dad wouldn't mind if we tore off the top half-sheets of plywood from the oat bin in the grain shed since the oats were low anyway. The plywood would make perfect sides for our flagship. We also took one of the little ladders the chickens use to strut in and out of the coop. That would be our plank. Bash thought about taking some chickens, too, but they don't behave well around water. Don't ask. We snatched a clothesline pole to be our mast. Bash ran up to his room to grab the sheets off his bed for a sail.

If the rest of our pirate gang pillaged and looted as much stuff from their homes, this would be the biggest—and weirdest—Pirate Fleet of the Pond ever built.

Chapter 14

The Pirate Pig of the Pond

The pirate crew reassembled on the shore of our pirate ocean. We'd littered the bank with bottles, boxes, bowls, bookends, bars of soap and even wooden picture frames, plus some volunteered crew in cages and a bucket of water.

Mary Jane yelled as she pedaled up. "Look! We had a couple plastic yacht toys at the store. I bought them with my allowance. I bet Christopher's mice can fit inside and steer."

"Wow!" Second Mate and Pirate Admiral Bash immediately promoted Mary Jane to third mate and assistant pirate admiral. I didn't care. I still was chief.

We nailed the sides onto our blue door floor flagship, anchored the mast into the middle to the left of the black door handle, and nailed Bash's bed sheet to the pole to catch a breeze. It sagged.

I flicked the droopy sheet. "How's it supposed to catch a breeze if there's only one pole and only one side is attached?"

"Um, because it's really a pirate flag, not a sail. We should draw a cool skull and crossbones on it."

"Your mom probably wouldn't like that."

"Well, if you squint just right, that stain where I spilled hot chocolate one night kinda looks like a skull and crossbones."

While Bash and I finished the flagship, the rest of the pirates split open sides of cereal boxes, carved openings into plastic bottles and planted handkerchief flags in shoeboxes and picture frames and whatever else we had for boats. After a while, we were ready.

Bash darted away. "Be right back."

A few minutes later, there he came, riding Captain Gulliver J. McFrederick the Third, an almost three-foot high, reddish barrel of sausages trotting on short, churning legs. The huge hog's ears drooped and his snout crinkled into an odd grin. Gulliver J. snuffled along, keeping his piggy nose to the ground in case he ran into something interesting to eat.

The Basher sat proudly on his stubby steed. "Pigs are smart. See, when I tug on his left ear, he turns left. When I tug on the right, he turns right. I tap him on the sides with my feet to go. Or I just yell 'giddyup.' I've almost taught him 'whoa' too."

"He doesn't throw you off?"

"Nah. Gulliver J. McFrederick the Third likes it. He follows me around the pigpen when I'm feeding him until I hop on. But sometimes on hot days he decides to roll in the mucky wallowing pool to cool off while I'm still aboard."

"Yuck."

Gulliver trotted right up and greeted the pirate gang.

Second Mate and Pirate Admiral Bash hopped off and stood with his hands on his hips. "Arrr, me hearties. Avast and anchors away. Shiver me timbers. Raise the giblets. See how the mainsail sets."

Sailor Jig scratched his head through his ball cap. "Huh?"

"Load up the crew."

"Oh."

Bonkers pulled his wagon load of pet cages onto the fishing pier and started packing mice into cups and the plastic yachts from Morris's Corner Store. "They've got the best ships of all, real ones."

"At least somebody will be safe," I muttered.

The bunnies commanded plastic-coated shoeboxes and plastic salad bowls. A garter snake ruled a 7-Up bottle.

Two white ducks, Martha and Mary, took position on two planks we tied together and equipped with washcloth sails mounted onto twigs and tiny tree branches. Buster the skunk stood on another plank ship, his tail fanned out above him like a black-and-white-striped sail.

Bonkers cuddled a raccoon. "This is Ralph. He's perfect for the wooden stool." Bonkers placed Ralph in the upside down stool that we'd wrapped in tin foil. Ralph stood on his hind feet, clamped little raccoon hands over the stool legs like they were pegs on a captain's wheel and stretched his masked face toward the pond. "See, he can't wait."

Bonkers tucked a newt into a ship built from a Cheerios box and wax paper. "They love the wading pool. I bet they think the pond is great." I hoped so. A Cheerios box probably would make for one soggy boat, even wrapped in plastic.

Jig and Jag loaded turtles and frogs into bottles, cans and boxes. The frogs barely could contain their enthusiasm and tried to launch without their ships, leaving Jig and Jag to hop around the pier, almost toppling off a time or two, as they stuffed frogs back inside their boats. They tried to get crickets to ride the sponge boats, but the crickets escaped in the middle of the confusion with the frogs.

Bash steered Captain Gulliver J. McFrederick toward the flagship, which Mary Jane and I were holding steady at the edge of the pier with a couple of strands of baling twine.

"Chief Assistant Swab Beamer, Pirate Capt. Gulliver J. McFrederick the Third says you are sailing with him on the flagship to lead his pirate flotilla."

"What! I thought you were going to sail the flagship."

Bash shook his head and saluted. "Nah, I'm the admiral."

I didn't return the salute. "And second mate.

"Beamer, I gotta stand on the pier and supervise the launching of the fleet. You're the chief. You sail."

"No way."

Third Mate and Assistant Pirate Admiral Mary Jane clucked her tongue. "Raymond William Boxby appears to be chicken. Maybe you better make him walk the chicken ladder plank."

"I'm not chicken!"

Jag snorted. "Boy. Big talk. Big fraidy-cat."

I spluttered and sputtered. "I'd love to sail. I live by the ocean, remember? It's just that I thought the honor should go to the admiral. It's his shed door . . . uh, pirate ship, after all."

About then, Captain Gulliver snuffled aboard the rocking ship, grunting his approval, though I suspect Bash had tossed an extra toasted cheese sandwich ahead of him.

Mary Jane crossed her arms. "Ha. Even a pig is braver than little boys like you."

None of them seemed to be in any hurry to sail, either. Still, a girl with a mouth as big as a cow's called me more fraidy-cat chicken than the pig. I wasn't afraid, just smart. Still . . .

I tentatively toed my way onto the pirate ship, which bobbed around wildly. Water splashed over my sneakers. A three-hundred-something-pound captain and ninety-something-pound boy might be too heavy something for a shed door on fence posts to float.

Bash pointed toward the center of the pond. "Pirates—*attack!*"

He and Mary Jane shoved the pirate flagship away from the pier. More water splashed over my sneakers. Gulliver grunted. I grabbed a plywood side and wobbled. "Um, guys."

"Don't worry, chief." Bash snatched up the chicken coop ladder gangplank and pushed us further into the pond. Jig, Jag and Bonkers began heaving ship upon ship into the waters after us. Uncle Jake barked furious encouragement as he jumped about the shoreline.

Pirate Admiral Bash pumped an imaginary sword. "Bonsai!"

The rest of the pirates danced and shouted on the shore. "Arrr! Woo hoo! Look at 'em go!"

If they wanted to play pirate, how come *I* was the only one on the water?

"Yikes." I slipped and crashed to my knees on the shed door. I tried to latch onto the coarse hairs of the captain's rust-colored back. The captain snuffled and squealed. Or perhaps it was me. I couldn't be sure.

Our flotilla probably had been under way for a good twenty seconds or so before the mutinies began. Mice poured out of the plastic yachts and drinking cups and dog-paddled the three feet to shore. Buster waved his sail tail right, then left, catching a breeze. Then he changed his mind, stepped off the ship and followed the mice.

Goo-Goo, Gee-Gee, and Ga-Ga bounded out of boxes and bowls. Turtles flopped off picture frames and bookends.

I steadied myself with one hand on the mast, the other on the captain's hog back. "Come back. Take me."

The garter snake slithered out of the 7-Up bottle and skimmed across the surface like a surfer riding a wave to the beach. With quacking so loud it drowned out my quaking, the ducks Martha and Mary hopped off their plank with the washcloth sail and raced each other to center of the pond. Ralph the raccoon tipped the stool, dove under water, surfaced with a fish in his paws and shot to shore with his feast.

The flagship bobbled. *"Yeow. Martha. Mary. Ralph. Tow me in."*

Finally, Captain Gulliver squealed, *"Rwheeeet, rwheeeet, rwheeeeet"* and dove off the aft of the flagship. The thrust shot the flag ship skipping past the middle of the massive pond toward the creek of doom. I wrapped my arms around the shaky mast and very calmly remarked, *"Aauughh! Aauughh! Aauughh!"* at the top of my lungs.

Pigs can swim. Mice can swim. Bunnies, turtles, raccoons, skunks, ducks, snakes, all can swim. Only one critter on the pond couldn't swim—me.

How close was I drifting to the far side of the pond, into Conneaut Creek and on out to the Atlantic Ocean? If I could steer this thing, I'd turn south and sail home to Virginia Beach. But I had no food for the trip. And I didn't want to go home sailing a shed door marked with pig hoof prints.

Nuts.

I tried to pull myself up the clothesline pole mast back to my feet. That's when the pirate ship flopped over—and kept turning. I scrambled alongside the capsizing ship as the bottom became the top. The excited pirates on shore launched a full-blown rescue operation.

"The mice! Pick up my mice before they run into the field. I don't want a fox to get them!" Bonkers shouted.

I bobbed up in time to see Jag scoop up a bunny and wrap it in her dress. "I've got Ga-Ga."

Jig dried another rabbit on his T-shirt. "It's Goo-Goo. Or is this one Gee-Gee?

Bash ran after the barreling barrow, frolicking in the cattails. "Gulliver, come here."

Mary Jane snuggled Buster while scanning the pond. "I want my boats."

"*Glub. Glub. Glub.*" That was me slipping under the wrong side of the ship. No one noticed. They were too busy apprehending the mutineers.

"*Bashh-glurp.*" I gagged and spat out pond water. My lungs burned. My ribs screamed. I plunged beneath the surface again. My T-shirt and jeans, too big now from all my running around on the farm all summer, soaked up heavy gallons of pond. Water streamed into my nose. I kicked my way up again, gasping, panting, burning, gagging.

Something bumped into my flailing legs.

Shark!

Uncle Rollie was right. Sharks. In the pond. I wouldn't have time to drown. I'd be eaten alive. *"Arrr!"*

"Woof!"

Woof? A barking shark with red hair? Not a shark, but . . .

I gasped. "Uncle Jake."

I abandoned ship and grabbed hold of masses of wet, red hair as Uncle Jake dog-paddled for the far shore, which now was nearer than the near shore. My knees bumped bottom as we hit the creek, which turned out to be pretty shallow. I staggered and crawled the rest of the way out of the water and flopped coughing and choking facedown onto the grass. Uncle Jake slurped my cheek, then ran off to herd a turtle back into the water.

I poked my glasses back into place, surprised that they stayed on. Three sponge boats—one red, one blue, and one green—floated down the creek, headed for the ocean. "Tell Mom I want to come home."

One of Bonkers's bunnies, maybe Gee-Gee, hopped up and burrowed itself between my shoulder and cheek. It shook water from its fur as I gasped and gagged some more. Now I knew why pirates were feared and hunted.

"Brutus! I mean Goo-Goo!" Bonkers ran up. "Woo-hoo! Ray-Ray found Goo-Goo. We can stop worrying now."

Bash trotted up astride Gulliver the Deserter. "How come you left our ship in the pond?"

"Actually, Raymond left all the ships in the pond." Mary Jane pointed out to sea. "Oops, another cereal box just sank. He's not a very good chief, is he?"

I screamed through a mouthful of grass and pond bank. *"Mmmrrrgghhaaarrrwwffffff!"*

Nobody believed me that I nearly drowned. On the phone that night, I begged Mom to fly me home before Bash and his lunatic friends decided to build a rocket car or a soybean bazooka or a bear trap that actually worked.

"Raymond, stop causing trouble," Mom said. "You're supposed to be helping your Aunt Tillie keep an eye on Bash. How could you let him use his bed sheets for a raft?"

Yeah, it's my fault my cousin's an idiot.

I sat on the back porch with Uncle Jake, staring at stars until I buried my face in Jake's shoulders to wipe the sweat streaming from my eyes. While it turned out that I didn't need any bandages, antiseptic, poison ivy cream, ice packs, tetanus shots, crutches, or—no thanks to the pirates—the possible tombstone, I found that I needed to add towels, cotton swabs, and a bilge pump for my lungs to my list of emergency supplies.

The screen door banged. The Basher shuffled out.

"Hey, Beamer."

I didn't say anything.

"I guess I didn't make such a great pirate captain." He sat on the other side of Uncle Jake.

"Duh."

We sat for a few seconds, not looking at each other.

"Ray."

"Yeah?"

"I'm sorry I didn't see you fall off the ship."

"Humpf."

Bash ruffled his hand through Uncle Jake's hair. "I didn't know you couldn't swim."

"Humpf."

Bash threw his arm around Uncle Jake. I yanked my hand away and crossed my arms. Bash perched his chin atop Uncle Jake's head and stared at me. "I could teach you."

"No way."

"Really, I can. I taught Gulliver J. McFrederick the Third."

"Pigs know how to swim."

Bash stared into the night sky.

"Ray."

"Yeah."

"It would have been awful if you'd drowned."

I glared at him. "I didn't think it sounded so great myself, Basher."

"It would have ruined the adventure."

"Humpf."

Bash scratched Uncle Jake's chin, then sat back. Uncle Jake lay down between us and yawned. Bash sighed. "It's more fun when you're here. I wish you could stay all the time."

"Why?"

Bash snatched a passing lightning bug and watched it glow green in his cupped hand before letting it go. "You're not afraid to play with me."

"Ha."

"But you do. You like adventures too."

I gripped the edge of the porch with both hands and let him have it. "I hate adventures! I hate this farm! I hate that you're always trying to kill me or break my bones or get your mom to yell at me! I hate that you boss me around even though I'm three months older than you! I hate this whole summer! I just want to go home and read my books and forget this ever happened!"

"Ray-Ray?" Bash's shoulders slumped as he bent down to look up at me.

"What?" I snapped.

"Swim lessons tomorrow?"

I brooded for a few moments. "Are you bringing the pig?"

"Nah."

"How 'bout Uncle Jake?"

"He can come."

"We're staying away from the creek that goes to the ocean?"

"The creek's not even deep enough to—"

"Are we staying away?"

"Well . . . sure."

I considered this. It would be something to do while I finished serving my sentence on this stupid farm. "Humpf. Maybe. Tomorrow. Or whenever Aunt Tillie ungrounds us."

Bash sat up. "Cool. You'll love swimming. Tomorrow. Or when we can. Anyway, it's bedtime now."

I stood up. "It's gonna be odd sleeping on mattresses with no sheets. I can't believe your mom is making us do that."

"Grown-ups can be weird sometimes."

"Yeah, *grown-ups* can be weird," I agreed, rolling my eyes.

Chapter 15

How I Became a Calf's Uncle

I hadn't expected to become an uncle so soon, but such is life in the country. Some critter or other has babies all the time on a farm. Kittens, chicks, piglets, ducklings, calves, and other animals, like Bash and his little sister, Darla, littered the place.

So I figured the upcoming summer calf might as well be under my protection. I'd learned a lot about surviving this nuthouse, and I figured I could help the newest inmate stay out of trouble. I needed somebody on my side.

About sixty dairy cows grazed about Uncle Rollie's farm,

and one of them, a red Jersey he called Callie, looked like she'd swallowed a water balloon with the hose still in it and the water still gushing.

Uncle Rollie sized her up. "Yep, she oughta deliver that calf within the week. Better put her in the box stall."

I poked Bash. "Deliver? What, like the mailman?"

The Basher rolled his eyes. "Pops means she's gonna give birth to a calf. That's why she's so fat. That's what you used to look like. Oh, a calf is a baby cow."

"I know what a calf is. I'm not that stupid. I'm smarter than you."

Bash leaned against one of the empty milking stalls and chewed on a piece of hay. "When a cow's gonna deliver, Pops puts her in a pen by herself. That way, the mama cow can take care of the calf without all the aunt cows fussing about."

I scraped cow gunk off the bottom of my sneakers and pulled again on my sagging jeans. Bash ran so much muscle off of me this summer that my pants barely stayed up. I whooshed right out of my trunks twice during swimming lessons last week. Good thing only Bash and Uncle Jake were at the pond with me.

I rubbed Callie's big belly. "So aunt cows are like people cows? I mean, people aunts?"

Bash grinned. "Only aunt cows don't try to pinch the calf's cheeks all the time or tell the mom how to dress it and feed it and stuff. I think aunt cows are easier."

Two mornings later, we headed out to the barn to help Uncle Rollie with chores. I hated getting up so early every single day, but checking on Callie helped me crawl out of bed in the mornings. She didn't make fun of me or try to talk me into going on dangerous missions. She didn't snicker when I slid baling twine through my belt loops to hold up my pants. Callie listened when I whispered whatever I wanted while I scratched the swirly part of her forehead hair or rubbed her soft, jiggly chin.

This morning, Callie shocked me. "Yuck. There's something gross sticking out her backside!"

Bash darted to the box stall and peered between the boards. "Cool. She's delivering." He yelled over his shoulder, "Pops, come quick!"

Uncle Rollie ambled over and leaned his arms on the top row of the box stall. Then he straightened. "Aw, horse feathers, it's breech." Uncle Rollie clambered over the pen wall.

Bash leaned against the pen and went into teacher mode. "Breech means that the calf is coming out backwards, feet first. It could get stuck. Pops is gonna turn it around."

"What about the horse feathers?"

Bash flicked my hair. "That means 'uh-oh.'"

I smashed my hair back in place and bopped his cap, popping it off his head. "So there are no horse feathers?"

Bash snaked out an arm, caught the cap without looking, twirled it, and zipped it back on his head as if he did that sort of thing all the time. But I saw the snicker in his eye. "Horses don't have feathers, Ray-Ray Sun . . . I mean, Beamer. Besides, these are cows."

I thunked his shoulder. "Stop calling me a sunbeam!"

Bash held up his hands. "I didn't. I mean, I started to but I stopped. You're Beamer." He shrugged.

"Or Ray. You could just say Ray." Ever since he nearly drowned me in the duck pond, Bash was trying to be less of a pain in the neck. I still didn't trust him.

Bash sat on the bottom board of the pen looking up at me. I knew he wanted to make a wisecrack. I could see the gleam in his eye as he struggled with it. He took off his cap and stared at it. "Ray's okay. But Beamer is better. It's more exciting, doncha think?"

I kicked at loose straw. But before I could tell the Basher what I thought, Uncle Rollie blurted, "Gotcha!" We snapped around in time to see him laying a slimy, gooey mess with four legs, a head and a tail onto the straw.

Bash jumped up and ran in circles. "All right! We're uncles!"

I stepped on the bottom board and leaned over the top. Callie nosed about the calf and licked the gunk off its skinny body. I thought I'd lose my breakfast right there. "Ew, *gross*."

"Sissy." Bash clamped his hand over his mouth. "Oops. Sorry."

I held my stomach. "Am not!"

"Well, it's not like cows have washcloths."

I took another peek and looked away. "Maybe we ought to give them some. *Blech*."

Callie licked that scrawny calf clean, leaving it a damp ruffle of reddish-tan hair on toothpick legs. Then she kept licking, as if trying to lift the thing up with her big, black tongue. Apparently, baby cows don't like mother's spit any more than boys do. "Mwaap." The calf swung its head this way and that, and tried to roll out of the way.

Finally, the little calf kneeled. The back legs flailed around a bit until they caught hold and stuck. Its tail end tottered in the air like a tree swishing in the wind. Callie swiped at the calf with another lick and down it tumbled.

Bash pumped his arm. "*Ka-boom!*"

I glared. "That wasn't nice."

The little thing clambered to its front knees, and staggered the back legs beneath it. It tapped around with the front, right hoof till it found solid ground beneath the straw, then repeated with the left. Slowly, and wobbling like a spun penny all twirled out and about to fall, the calf stood.

Bash leaped to the bottom board of the box stall beside me. "Yahoo! Claudeenetta's up!"

I looked at him. "Claudeenetta?"

"Yeah. Claudeenetta Louisa."

I studied the quavering mini-cow. "How do you know it's a she?"

Bash whapped me with his ball cap. "Don't you know anything?"

"Well, she's awfully tiny for such a big name."

"You got something better, Beamer?" Bash challenged.

"What about . . . Amy!"

"Amy?" I could see him snickering. I didn't care.

"Yeah. I think she looks more like an Amy—tiny and pretty—than a Claudeenetta, whatever that is. I've never even heard of a Claudeenetta."

That did it. Bash couldn't hold it in anymore. "Aww, does widdle Way-Way think the baby moo cow is pwetty?"

"You're a pig-nosed possum breath."

The Basher hooted and almost fell off the box stall board. Before I could push, he caught himself. "I know. We'll name her Claudeenetta Louisa Amelia Jones. Amelia's short for Amy."

"Where'd Jones come from?"

"A kid at school. His face kinda looks like a cow's."

"Oh."

Bash leaped to the ground and dashed for the grain barrels. I turned to the pen and whispered to Little Miss Wobbly, "Good morning, Amy."

While Amy got about the business of figuring out where her first meal was coming from, we filled feed boxes as Uncle Rollie attached milking machines to the rest of the cows. We lugged pails of water, along with hay and grain to Callie too.

"Warm water, first, boys," Uncle Rollie called out. "It helps after birthing. Then cold like usual."

I leaned on the box stall again and watched. Amy sprawled on the straw, resting after her first meal, which she got by poking beneath Callie's udder. Now Callie lumbered around the pen, nearly stepping on her calf a dozen or so times. I cringed.

"Ah, she won't step on her calf." Bash slid the empty grain box out of the pen. "They know where their kids are all the time. She's a mom."

Still, I had about sixteen heart attacks as Callie ate.

Over the next two days, Amy worked out the kinks. She scampered around the pen like a gymnast warming up, her big brown eyes blinking and stubby black nose testing the air. She looked like a fawn without the spots. The reddish-tan hair on top of her head swirled into a couple of tiny curls as white as Aunt Tillie's bed sheets.

I'd climb into the pen and wrestle with her. Once, Amy—I just couldn't call her Claudeenetta—grabbed a mouthful of my shirt and started chewing. I yanked it back from her. She butted me with her head, which I found surprisingly hard. She bleated a "Mwaap" at me when I left, asking for more. But I had a headache.

Uncle Rollie said Amy would stay in the stall with Callie for three days. After that, Callie would go back out to the pasture and Amy would move into a calf hutch—like a big doghouse—where we'd start feeding her calf formula.

That night, with Bash sentenced to drying supper dishes, I sneaked out to the barn to have another tussle with Amy to help her celebrate being two-and-a-half days old. We'd been grounded nine days ago after the adults found out where the rest of the Pirate Pig's flotilla came from, and the barn was about the furthest we could wander from the house, and only then to do chores. I figured checking on the calf counted. I flipped on the barn lights.

I froze.

Amy lay still in the middle of the pen, her legs stretched

out stiff, her belly puffed out, her little neck arched, her eyes scrunched closed.

"Amy! What's wrong?"

She didn't move at first. Then her tiny head jerked.

Callie nuzzled Amy's ribs and her white underbelly. She fretted around the box stall, stepping over the prone calf, bumping her with her foot now and then. And she looked at me with those huge, brown eyes. "Do something," Callie's eyes said.

I did. I ran for the house, screaming like crazy. Yeah, I know, not cool, but it was something. "Bash! *Basher!* Am . . . Claudeenetta's sick! Claudeenetta's sick! *Come quick!*"

Bash yanked on his sneakers and sprinted to the barn. For once, I almost kept up with him. He scrambled over the boards of the pen and checked Amy. Cold ears. They're supposed to be warm. Dry nose. It's supposed to be wet. Bash pried open her mouth as best as he could. He didn't see anything caught past her tiny teeth.

Slowly, Bash stood up, staring down at Amy while rubbing Callie's side. He chewed his tongue. He didn't say anything.

I couldn't take it any longer. "What do we *do*?"

Bash shrugged. "Dunno. Finish doing dishes until Ma and Pops get home from the Gobnotters's farm, I guess. They said they'd be right back after dropping off some eggs."

"But Amy . . . Claudeenetta Louisa Amelia Jones is sick. Call them."

"They'll be right back, Beams."

"Call the cow doctor. We can't wait."

Bash climbed over the box stall boards and jumped to the ground with a thud. "The vet won't come out this late. She's just a calf. We have others."

I grabbed him by the shoulders. "What do you mean she's *just* a calf! You don't have any other . . . Amys!"

Bash glanced into my face, then looked down at his sneakers. "I'm teasing, Beamer. I don't remember the vet's number. I'm trying to think." He chewed harder on his tongue.

I let go of Bash and looked over the stall. "Think faster, then!"

"Well, stop yelling, then!" Bash slumped against the boards. His lower lip trembled. My eyes were starting to sweat, but I didn't want Bash to see because he'd probably make fun of that too. But I couldn't think of anything, either. You don't give cows Tylenol or Mylanta. Do you?

"Do you give cows Tylenol or Mylanta?"

Bash grinned. "I gave one a Popsicle once. Ma told me not to give them anything from the house anymore. Too bad 'cause the cow liked the Popsicle. It was strawberry."

I tried to snap my fingers, which I'd never learned to do. I punched a fist into the palm of the other hand instead. "Bonkers! Call Bonkers. He'll know."

"Can't." Bash didn't move from the side of the pen. "His whole family is on a missions trip with his church. Jig and Jag are taking care of his animals."

"Not you? You live closer."

"When they went on vacation last year, I did watch their animals. I wanted to see if a tortoise really could beat a hare in a race. I fished all his turtles out of their pond and pulled all his rabbits from their pen and lined them up." Bash slowly shook his head. "Beamer, I don't think the story about the tortoise and the hare is true. The turtles were the only things I could catch without help."

While Bash rambled on, I worried myself sick, Callie kept stepping around Amy's still body. "Bash, we need to get Amy out of there."

"I know. But if we knock the boards off one side of the box stall, Callie will wander off. And Claudeenetta Louisa Amelia Jones already is too heavy for me to pass over the top board. And you couldn't catch her."

"Could too. I'm just as strong as you. Stronger. You couldn't get her up that far."

Bash pushed himself away from the box stall and looked at Amy. Her head twitched. Bash cringed. "Well, anyway, you're not supposed to move injured people unless you're with the ambulance squad. Hey, let's drag her under the bottom board."

I dug my fingers into the top board. "Real good, Basher. Ambulance people do that all the time. Just grab the sick guy by the feet and pull him across the room. What about a stretcher, huh?"

Bash looked around and shrugged. "We don't have a stretcher."

Amy shuddered. I jumped. "Yes we do." I ran to the pile of empty feed sacks and snatched a burlap bag. I sprinted back to the pen and we both shot over the boards. As gently as we could, we lifted and dragged Amy's cold, rigid body onto the feed sack. Then we pulled the sack with her riding on it underneath the bottom board.

I knelt beside my calf. "Told you."

Then Amy began to shiver. Her stick legs stuck out straight and stiff. Her puffed-up belly shook. She tried to cough but couldn't. She opened her eyes, looked up at us, made a weak, baby cow "maaww" sound, then closed her eyes again.

I saw fear in Bash's eyes. "Beamer, she's dying!"

Chapter 16

A Quilt, a Calf, and a Prayer for a Cure

Amy's little calf body shuddered. Like I'd done a few moments earlier, Bash wiped sweat from his eyes. He shuddered too. Or maybe it was me.

"Ray-Ray, put some hay bales around her like a fence to protect her. I'll be right back."

Bash ran back into the barn in two minutes, holding a phone and dragging the quilt from his mom and dad's bed behind him. "Claudeenetta needs it."

I folded that big blanket over Amy's little body three or four times. Then I squished it in good around her on the bed of straw I spread for her on the barn floor. "C'mon, girl, get better!"

Bash paced around the hay bale fence, the phone clamped to his ear. "Pops must've left his phone in the truck again. This one's Ma's." He slammed the phone shut. "What's taking Ma and Pops so long?"

I perched on one of the bales and watched the patient. Bash ran from the barn. He dashed back inside a minute or two later, carrying a radio, a scrap of paper, and a Hershey's bar. He handed me the chocolate. "Here. Doctors need their strength. Uncle doctors."

Bash dug the cell phone from his pocket and held up the ripped paper. "Had to find Jig and Jag's phone number."

I watched him punch in numbers. "Jig and Jag get to have cell phones?"

"No. It's their house number." Bash listened. "Busy. How come they don't have call waiting like normal people?"

I nibbled at the candy but left the radio off. Bash held the phone and watched Amy. I'd never seen either Bash or Amy this still.

"She's so tiny, isn't she, Raymond?"

"Yeah."

Amy shivered. Bash dropped the phone into his pocket. "They never leave me alone for more than ten minutes, even when I beg them. I guess they figured with you here, they could."

"Yeah, fat lot of good letting me be in charge has done so far this summer."

Bash paced. "Ma said when they left that they'd be back in five minutes and not to get into any trouble and to listen to you. She must have been kidding about that last part."

My stomach flipped and flopped as Amy's belly quivered. "Does God hear prayers for cows?"

Bash took off his ball cap and twisted it. "Sure. Pops prays for everything. I've heard him pray for the crops, the tractor, the bills, the house. He prays for me. A lot."

"Does he pray for cows?"

Bash fitted his cap back onto his straw hair. "I've heard him thank God for every new cow, including when Claudeenetta Louisa Amelia Jones was born. Don't you remember family devotions that day after dinner?"

"Kinda. That's the day he read us something about God caring for sparrows."

Bash nodded. "Sparrows are pesky birds. But God knows every one of 'em. He watches everything He made."

I glanced around the barn ceiling looking for sparrows. "So nothing's too silly to pray about?"

Bash dug his hands into his pockets. "Spelling tests. That never works."

"Don't you still have to do your part? Study?"

"I could try that . . ."

Amy jerked.

"Um, God?" I prayed. "Thank you for my little Amy. But she's sick. Please make her better."

Praying felt strange. I didn't do it except for over dinner and if Mom made me at bedtime. And for spelling tests,
though that didn't work for me, either. But maybe prayer
would work on cows. Maybe cows were like big sparrows.

Bash knelt down and propped his elbows on a hay bale.
"It's me again, God. Show us what to do. We're her uncles."

"Thank you, God." I looked up. I didn't see God. Just a
bunch of fly gunk on the barn ceiling. I hoped He could see
through it.

Maybe God would listen to Bash. I didn't think God
would bother with me.

Amy shivered. It wasn't just the normal shakes a cow
sometimes gets after guzzling five pails of water. Her whole
body shook like an angry rooster. Her neck arched, her teeth
clenched tightly when she wasn't coughing, and her eyes
scrunched up real hard.

"Amy!" Bash yelled. Wow. He'd called her by the name I
gave her. "Beamer, she's in trouble! What do we do?"

"Me? You're the farm boy. You're the guy who says he
knows God. I tried it out and look, she's worse!"

Amy's breathing turned real raspy. I snatched the comforter off Amy and started trying to get my arms around her.
"We're going to do the Heidrich maneuver."

"The what?"

Amy felt like dead weight. "The Heidrich maneuver.
That thing you do on people who are choking. You get
behind them, put double fists below their rib cage and yank
up real fast."

Bash jumped up. "Oh, the *Heimlich* maneuver. We learned
about it in health class."

"Whatever. Just help me figure out where to put my fists."

I had an arm slipped beneath her side. I joined my hands. Bash tried to pull her up as much as he could while I felt under her stomach. Oh, no. I remembered that cows have *four stomachs! Now what? Find one and go.*

I felt the rib cage and slid my hands down until I ran out of ribs. I stretched out over her back until I had Amy in a big bear hug. Then I yanked my fists into her gut.

"Mwaap." Amy coughed.

"Another one!" EMT Basher yelled.

I did it again. Stomach Number Two? Amy coughed harder. One more time. Fire Three! Hard.

"Mwaaap!" Amy gagged. And burped. And something that looked like a crumpled ball of hay rolled out of her mouth. Other stuff came out too. Yuck! I almost threw up, too, but Aunt Tillie's quilt seemed messy enough without my help.

Amy sucked in a deep breath. So did we. She looked around and wobbled to her feet. I hugged her so hard she almost started choking again. She coughed and breathed and pounced around the hay pen, tiny hooves tearing into Aunt Tillie's quilt.

"Thank you, God!" I gasped through giggles as I tried to pull the quilt from beneath her tumbling feet.

"Yep." Uncle Bash shook some straw off the blanket before dropping it back to the floor.

Maybe God did care about sparrows and cows. Or was He just up there somewhere eating popcorn and watching us do all the work that really saved Amy?

Bonkers told us a few days later that maybe the ball of hay had gotten stuck in Amy's throat and it was slowly choking her. Some air could get by, but eventually it would work its way down to snuff her out. Or maybe something she nibbled on made her sick. Or maybe she just didn't want to be squeezed anymore, so she jumped up to get away. He told us he'd be going to vet school in about eight more years and he'd let us know then and send us a bill.

Right then, we didn't know what had happened and we didn't care. We had our cow niece back.

Amy leaped for a hay bale, but only made it halfway over. She teetered, her front legs dangling over one side and her hind legs dangling over the other, like she was caught sideways on a balance beam. She looked back at us, bleating, "Maaawwww."

We fell onto the comforter and laughed.

Which is when the barn door opened and Uncle Rollie and Aunt Tillie walked in.

Uncle Rollie stared down at us and scratched his head through his cap. "Ol' Gobby and I got to talking about our corn crops—"

"And baseball," Aunt Tillie said.

"—and baseball, and I just noticed as we pulled into the drive that I had fifteen new messages on my phone, which I left in the truck, and—"

Aunt Tillie's eyes bugged out. She grabbed Uncle Rollie's shoulder and launched herself in front of him. "Is that Grandma Hinglehobb's quilt? On the barn floor? What . . . what . . . what . . . We can't even leave you hooligans for twenty minutes while we're just two houses away, right in plain sight, and yet you still . . . you still . . . Roland! Those boys . . ."

Bash ran up to her. "Ma, Ray's a hero! He saved Claud . . . He saved *Amy's* life. He finally got it all right."

"What do you mean 'finally?'" I shoved him down onto the quilt.

"Boys." Uncle Rollie said the word quietly, barely above a whisper. But we heard trouble. We stopped rolling around.

Uncle Rollie took Aunt Tillie's arm. His voice remained unnaturally calm. "I'm taking Mattie, here, to the house. I will be back in five minutes. Try to have your story straight by then. I can hardly wait."

Time to pray again.

"Mwwwaaaaap?" Amy asked.

I knelt down and helped her off the hay bale. "Yep. I think we accidentally fell into trouble again."

Uncle Bash ruffled Amy's noggin. "But your Uncle Beamer still is a hero. He saved your life." He rubbed his chin and said, "Amy. That is a kinda cool name. Short, but okay."

I traced the white hair just behind her stubby, black nose. "Um, Amy, can we sleep out here with you tonight? It might save our lives."

"Maaawwwww!"

"Thanks." We started rolling up Aunt Tillie's quilt while we waited for Uncle Rollie to return for us two heroes.

Chapter 17

Gone Fishin'

"You know what we haven't done yet?"

I looked up from my comic book and cringed at Bash leaning over me, bouncing on his toes in expectation of an answer. I groaned. "Flown giant kites off the grain silos? Rigged the corn picker to launch chickens in Superman capes? Arm-wrestled Mary Jane for free shoulder punches?"

The Basher popped up and paced between our beds. "Awesome ideas, Beamer. All except that last one. My arm stung for two weeks the last time I lost a game of free hits to Mary Jane."

I let the comic book flop to my chest. "So what torture do you have in mind for me?"

"Not torture. Nearly the whole summer has passed and I haven't taught you how to fish."

"How tragic."

Bash put on the brakes and leaned over me again. "You'll like it. It's your kinda thing. You sit and watch the day go by. You can even take your comic books with you."

I propped myself up on my elbow. "Really?"

"Yep. It's practically boring, just what you've been begging for."

Ever since he nearly drowned me in the duck pond, Bash pestered me night and day with his idea of kindness. I almost wished he'd go back to tormenting me with his stupid stunts.

"You're not just trying to torment me with another stupid stunt, are you?"

Bash shook his head so hard I thought I heard the rocks rattling. "Nope. We hardly ever catch any sharks anymore. A killer octopus once in a while, but hardly any sharks. Not full-grown ones, anyway."

I sat up. "Hold it. I thought you said those were bluegill nipping at my toes during swimming lessons."

"Kidding. The duck pond's not big enough for sharks. I already asked Pops. C'mon, Beamer, grab your comic books and let's get the rods. And worms."

Bash flew out the bedroom door. I sighed. I crawled out of bed and collected the stash of comic books I'd smuggled to the farm in my suitcase. Why hurry? We still were grounded for messing up Aunt Tillie's dumb ol' quilt a week ago. It was now the end of July and we'd spent most of it in prison.

At least Amy was fine. And we wouldn't be allowed to go fishing.

I clunked down the stairs just in time to hear Aunt Tillie lecturing Bash. "Just try not to drown your cousin this time." *Nuts. I couldn't even count on staying grounded when I needed it most. We were going fishing.*

I followed Bash to the tool shed. He climbed the work-bench to wrestle fishing poles from nail hooks on the wall. He pulled a shovel out of a barrel full of rakes, brooms, and axes in the corner, and pushed it into my hands.

I looked at the shovel. "What's that for?"

"Bait."

"How come I get the shovel?"

From the sideboard behind the barrel, Bash picked up an empty soup can. "'Cause I have to carry the worm wagon."

"That's a tin can," I said. But Bash already had shot out of the tool shed. I trudged after him, dragging the shovel behind me. At the edge of the garden, Fisherman Bash held up his hand like the leader of an expedition halting the troops. "Dig here."

"It's your shovel. You dig,"

Bush held up the tin can. "Can't. I'm holding the worm wagon. If I don't hold the worm wagon, how are we going to capture the worms?"

I rolled my eyes, poked my glasses up my nose, then rammed the shovel into the ground. Not much happened. I stomped on the top rim and it bit down a bit. I turned over some ground. No worms. I kept plodding.

A worm. Before Bash made a snatch at it, the worm

sucked itself further into the earth. I wheeled on him. "Why didn't you grab it?"

"You're the digger and catcher. I'm holding the worm wagon."

"This snow shovel you gave me doesn't dig well at all."

"Oops." Bash pushed the tin can in my other hand and dashed to the tool shed. Once he ran back with the pointy-ended shovel, I turned over dirt loaded with whole colonies of slimy, gooey worms. I'm surprised they hadn't tangled them-selves into one big worm ball, they were so thick. I grabbed a glob and plopped them into the soup can.

"Add some dirt," Bash said as I wiped wormy gunk onto my baggy jeans. I topped the can with dirt, then wiped my hands again.

Bash trotted toward the pond. "I'll get the rods ready while you put away the shovels."

"Why do I have to put away the shovels?"

Bash called over his shoulder, "'Cause Ma will ground us again if you leave them there."

"That's not what I meant." But Fisherman Bash had already rounded the barn.

Uncle Jake sat beside me, thumping his bushy tail on the garden. I scratched his ears. "How do I get into these things, Uncle Jake? I'm the older cousin. I'm the smarter cousin. I'm the one who's supposed to be in charge and keep us out of trouble. So how does the little squirrel brain keep outfoxing me?"

Uncle Jake slurped my face with his big, wet doggy tongue, jumped up and scampered toward the pond. Within seconds, Uncle Jake, bushy tail and all, disappeared behind the barn.

"Traitor!"

I dragged the shovels to the tool shed and considered sneaking back to the bedroom. But Bash also had the comic books in a backpack that included sandwiches and bananas. We used the backpack because I'd ripped all the pockets out of my jeans carrying nails, rocks, and other jagged oddities in Bash's other schemes. No wonder I'd lost so much weight—I was Bash's pack mule. Now I couldn't carry anything, not even good dirt clods to throw.

I kicked a rock out of the driveway, then stomped off to the pond. When I clomped onto the pond pier, Bash handed me one of the fishing poles.

"They are *not* fishing poles," he lectured. "They are rods with spinner reels."

Oh, great. Bash's helpful teacher mode.

Bash picked up the other pole. "If you cast right, you can reach the other side of the pond. What you do is hold your rod in front of you like this. Now turn that crank on the spinner—the other way—until the bobber hangs a bit below the tip. You're ready."

The red and white ball dangled from the fish line. Below it swung a hunk of lead Bash called the sinker. A hook curled at the end of the line.

Bash pointed at the spinney thing. "See that button on the reel? Press that and hold it in."

"Nothing happened."

"It's not supposed to yet. Not till you release it. It's like a video game."

Video games usually don't include really sharp hooks and insane cousins.

"Now raise up your arm so the rod's straight up, bend your wrist back so the rod's way behind you . . . and swing. Flick your wrist and let go of the release button. *Wheeeee!*"

Bash's line zipped across the pond in a fluttery arc, splashing down nearly on the other side, almost to the creek. The red and white ball disappeared for a moment, then bobbed up. Bash began reeling the line back in with steady turns of the spinner crank. "See? Easy. Say, where's your line?"

"Stuck to the cuff of my jeans, I think. The hook snagged my pants on the back swing."

Bash's eyes widened. "That coulda hurt. I've hooked my ear before and Pops's twice. C'mon, we gotta practice."

"Can I borrow your ball cap? I wanna pull it over my ears before your next throw."

"Cast," Fisherman Bash corrected.

Bash's casts continued to sail across the pond. My pole—rod, whatever—slapped the water on the next cast. A couple tries later, I almost had the motion but the line stayed stubbornly on the reel.

Bash slapped his hand over his mouth but could not clamp off the chortles. When he finished laughing, he pointed at my pole. "Beamer, hold that button, swing, flick, let go of the button and watch the line fly."

I yanked my rod away. "I'm not a moron."

"The evidence, ladies and gentlemen of the jury . . ."

"Go eat a worm!"

Another laughing fit swamped Bash.

I pressed the release button. I held up my arm. I bent back my wrist. I swept. I flicked. I released. Hook, line, sinker and bobber dropped straight down in front of me, ker-plop, into the cattails around the pier.

"Okay." Bash coughed into his sleeve. "I think we're ready to bait the hooks and begin fishing."

"So why are we trying to throw our lines to the other side of the pond in the first place?"

Bash dug into the dirt in the soup can. "'Cause that's where the fish are."

"Then why don't we just walk over and use the fishing pier on that side?"

Bash pulled out a worm that stretched like a rubber band and sighed. "You don't know anything about fishing, Beamer. The fish are always where you're not. If we went over there, they'd come over here."

"How do they know?"

"They know. So we always have to cast to the other side. It's in the Farmin' and Fishin' Book."

I rolled my eyes.

We sat on the edge of the fishing pier, the can of worms between us. We each scrunched a worm onto our hook—I only jabbed myself twice—and zipped our lines out into the pond. Mine went a good four or five feet this time. Since Bash's went a great deal further, I reeled my line in slowly, red and white bobber drifting along without doing any bobbing.

"Are there any fish in there besides those toe-nipping bluegill?"

Bash nodded, not taking his eyes off his bobber. "Sure. Some largemouth bass that are tricky to catch. Maybe a catfish or two. And whatever swims in from the creek, like killer whales and stuff. Pops says they struck a spring when they dug the pond, so most anything is possible."

"Except sharks?"

"And electric eels. I asked for those too."

"Good."

We cast again. I adjusted my throw now that we were sitting down. I hooked a plank or two before Bash showed me a sidearm cast. My line wobbled about halfway out into the pond before ker-plunking into the water. Bash's zipped nearly to the creek.

The bobbers didn't bob.

Fisherman Bash rocked back and rubbed his chin. "The problem is that we left something out."

"What?"

"Philosophizing."

I stared at him. "Fill-oss-o-fa-whoing?"

Bash's line click-click-clicked around the reel. "Philosophizing. It means figuring out the answers to all the questions no one asked."

"That makes as much sense as a box of rocks."

Bash swatted at a buzzing dragonfly. "Fish won't bite unless they hear philosophizing. You start."

"I don't want to figure out anything. And you don't care what I think, anyway."

"Sure I do. You're my cousin. And I wanna catch a whopper, so you gotta ask big questions."

I huffed. "So what do people philosophize about?"

"Pops and his buddies yak about dumb laws Congress makes. Nutty things women do. Religion and how to live right. That sort of thing."

Congress sounded too much like doing social studies homework in the summer. Girls were . . . I dunno. I didn't know why I'd want to talk to Bash about girls. Church stuff— I was getting pretty fed up with that. "Ah, forget it, Bash. Just fish."

"Can't. You need to philosophize."

"You start."

Bash shook his head. "You always say you're the smart one, and the smarties think they know everything. That's what philosophizing is all about."

"I am the smart one."

"Prove it. Say something stupid."

I wondered if I could whap Bash with my fishing pole. "Okay, dummy, how come there are so many different churches?"

Bash grinned and lined up his pole for another cast. "'Cause we wouldn't all fit in one building."

I knew I was the smart one. "See, you don't know. I mean, you guys go to Laughing Brook Bible Church. Bonkers goes to Grace AME. There's a Presbyterian church across the street from us back home, and a Lutheran church the next block over. If there's only one God, why so many churches?"

Bash whizzed his line across the pond. "Aw, grown-ups make it hard. I just talk to God and He tells me."

I shook my head. "I thought you were mumbling to yourself because you'd gone nuts."

My bobber danced. It didn't go under, but it moved. Huh. Maybe philosophizing worked. We both reeled in empty hooks. Bash stared into the water like he could see to the bottom. "It's a bluegill. They're sneaky. They steal worms."

We rebaited. I only stabbed myself once this time. "Well, there are a bunch of churches and they've got a bunch of different rules."

"God wrote down His rules in the Farmin' and Fishin' Book."

We reeled in the lines and cast again, almost tangling lines.

Bash pointed his pole. "You fish on that side. I'll cast on the other side where the fish are. Ha!"

I tossed off a sideways cast but dipped my pole too low. The hook snagged a glob of pond scum around the cattails behind us and I sent it sailing out to middle of the pond, where it hit with a ker-splash. Bash laughed so hard he wobbled onto his side.

I banged the handle of the pole on the pier. "Cut it out. I bet you couldn't snag pond scum and throw it out there like that."

"Wouldn't want to." But on his next three casts, I spotted him aiming for it. He missed every time. I had done it without trying.

Then I saw my bobber bob. A fish nibbling! Enough scum. Gotta keep Bash philosophizing so the fish keep biting. "How come you keep calling the Bible a farming and fishing book? That's stupid. The Bible's not about farming or fishing."

"Sure it is. We gotta grow the fruit of the Spirit, like peace and love and goodness and kindness and all that stuff."

"Fruit is apples or bananas or oranges."

Bash slowly cranked his spinner, drawing the string across the pond for the fish to chase. "We don't grow bananas or oranges in Ohio."

"You know what I mean, rhubarb head."

"Abraham, Jacob, Job, David—lots of guys were farmers. We farmers understand fruit talk and other stuff in the pages, like planting seeds and separating sheep from goats."

"And boys from their brains."

Bash watched his bobber bobble on the pond. "Jesus's best friends, Peter, James, and John, were fishermen. And Jesus said we're supposed to be fishers of men. And grow fruits. See? Farmin' and fishin'. *Woo-Wee!*"

Something yanked Bash's bobber under water. Bash jerked the rod, then cranked the spinner while hooting and hollering. "I got one! I got one!" The string came out of the water with a flat, five-inch fish with a bluish tinge around the gills wriggling at the end. Bash snatched the line and swung the flapping fish toward him. He slid it through his cupped hands, pushing the dorsal fin full of sharp little knife points backward, like petting a cat. "Pretty bluegill, ain't she?"

I leaned in close. "Cool. What do they taste like?"

"Pretty good fried in a pan." Bash popped the hook out of the bluegill's mouth and tossed it back into the pond. I gasped at the widening rings in the water. "What'd you do that for?"

"Catch and release."

I thunked his shoulder. "We can't eat released fish."

Bash didn't look up from rebaiting his hook. "Have you ever had to clean a fish? It's messy, yucky, and Ma will make us do it. If we wait for Pops to catch some bass on Saturday, he'll clean 'em and we can eat 'em."

"So what are we fishing for?"

Fisherman Bash shrugged. "It's fun."

"Not for the fish."

"Cast, Beamer."

Nuts. I reloaded from the soup can and whooshed the line as hard as I could. It unstrung more than halfway across the pond this time. Cool. But the bobber didn't bob. I tried to think of something else that would make my weirdo cousin philosophize a fish onto my hook.

"How come I gotta go to church? It's not like I'm as bad as Tommy 'The Snot' Snoggins. I bet even his own mom can't stand him."

"You haven't been harvested."

I watched my unbobbing bobber. "I'm not a soybean."

"You sure? You kinda look like one. I think it's your ears."

"Your head is stuffed with hay. And you don't have gray cells, you have purple clover cells."

Bash hooted. "Good one. Anyway, Beamer, when Pops plants oats, he wants oats. So if a big ol' grapevine grows up in the middle of the field, Pops is gonna rip it out."

Did the bobber jiggle? Was a philosophical fish sniffing at the worm? I had to keep Bash preaching. "Why not take the oats and grapes?"

"Because grain uses oats, not grape juice."

We reeled in our lines. The worms were gone. The Basher dug out another slimer and passed the soup can before scratching his head through his baseball cap. He held the worm in his scratching hand. We scrunched worms onto the hooks and side-armed casts across the pond.

Bash started reeling in. "Remember our memory verse from Sunday? The one in Matthew 6:33. It said to seek God's kingdom first and you get all the other stuff too."

I watched my bobber drift back to me as I cranked the clicking reel. "Wasn't the one from the week before about the top commandment being loving the Lord with all your heart, soul, and clover brains and number two is love the person next door like he was you?"

"Ray-Ray Sunbeam Beamer, you were listening! Yep, Matthew Chapter 22. I remember it was Matthew because it wasn't John—"

That made no sense.

"—and 22 because of the double twos for the two commandments. But I forgot the verse."

"Not such a Bible showoff now, are you?" I whipped another cast across the pond. Ha! Almost landed that one on the opposite bank. Bash cast. His line flew in a slow, lazy arc that nearly overshot the pond before plopping into the water.

"I remember that if you're not His friend, Jesus will say, 'Go away. I don't know you.' His guard angels throw you out into the darkness. That's in the Farmin' and Fishin' Book. Look it up."

Throw me out? I hate the dark.

Oh, no. I wasn't letting Bash pull that Sunday school junk on me. I bet that cold glob of squishy pond scum feeling would go away as soon as I escaped this stupid farm with all these crazy dorky, fish-faced . . .

"*Wow!*" Bash punched my arm. The crank jumped out of my fingers and the reel turned the other way on its own. A fish—a big one—held my line!

Chapter 18

Caught By a Philosophical Fish

My bobber plunged with a *"glub."*

Bash pumped his fist. "Yank it! Yank it!"

I locked the line and jerked. Something tugged back. "It's taking my fishing pole!"

"Rod. It's a rod and reel, not a fishing pole."

The fish nearly ripped the pole from my hands. "It's going to be a submarine if you don't help!"

Bash grabbed me around the waist and dug in his heels. I

cranked the reel. I nearly fell backward when a long, skinny fish slashed out of the water with my line. Bash let go and stumbled. "Wow. A rainbow trout! How'd you do that?"

I clamped a tighter grip on the pole. Rod. Whatever. "Quit philosophizing and help!"

Bash locked his arms around me again and held on. I reeled. The trout fought. I yanked. Bash latched onto the pole with me. The trout flipped and flapped. I cranked. Bash lugged. The trout swung into the air. I tumbled into Bash. We both slammed backward onto the dock. The flying trout splatted on top of us.

I dropped the pole and grabbed at the trout. "Gotcha." It squirted through my hands. I tried to trap it against Bash's belly.

"Woooaaaaaaoooowwww!" he whooped as nearly a foot and a half of wet fish flopped underneath his T-shirt.

"Come back." I fished beneath Bash's shirt for the wriggling trout. Bash reached down through his collar as I clawed upward. When both our hands hit him, the trout slapped his tail and shot out the neck of Bash's T-shirt. The fish flopped to the pier, the line trailing behind.

We both scrambled to our feet. I circled Bash and lunged at the trout, which lay still on the pier. "Got it. Whoops." I tripped over the line, then the rod. Bash stumbled over my feet. The reel, no longer locked, click-click-clicked as he dropped, unraveling the line still snaking up under the front of his T-shirt.

"Get the trout . . . *ouch*." Bash crashed to the pier on top of his pole.

I finally scooped the winded trout against my chest. His flank sparkled bits of green and purple in the sunlight as we all gasped for a few seconds. "What do I do with him?"

Bash crawled to his knees, trying to unwrap the line from himself. "Unhook him."

"How?"

"Well, put him somewhere safe and unwind me and I'll unhook him." String circled Bash six or seven times and the rod clattered between his feet. I looked for a place to set the trout and finally just stuffed it part way into my jeans pocket.

Suddenly, I remembered my pockets had no bottoms. A slimy trout dropped right through the hole and slid down a baggy leg to my knee. *"Yi-yi-yi-yi-yi-yiiiiiiiiiii!"* The trout wriggled to my calf, slipped out the bottom of my pants and onto the pier.

I tried to hop the creepy feeling off my leg. "Yuck. My leg is covered in fish slime."

Bash ducked and rolled to keep from being stomped on during my fish slime dance. "Stop jumping." The Basher tried to bash me with the fishing pole, which was hard to do considering how much I hopped and how tightly miles of fish string pinned his arms to his sides.

And then the string tethered us together.

The whole sequence took about fifteen seconds, maybe twenty. The trout lay on the pier, staring up at me, still hooked to my fishing line. The line from the fish ran around both of us a few times, circled Bash a few times more, shot up my pant leg, out my pocket, snaked up to the neck of Bash's shirt, down his belly and to the pole, which by now Bash and

I had exchanged about seventeen times as we tried to beat each other with it while it looped, circled, dodged and dived all around our bodies.

We were about as close as two cousins could ever want to be. Our noses were jammed into in each other's armpits.

"Cut bait," I snuffled into Bash's armpit.

"The trout has the bait." Bash's breath tickled my armpit.

"Then cut trout."

"Maybe I can reach my pocketknife if we twist around like this . . ."

"*Yikes! Watch out!* We almost toppled off the pier."

Bash spoke into my armpit again. "Beamer, can you move your legs?"

I tried to kick. "Nope. They're tied up in fish line. You?"

Bash struggled against me. "Same here. Okay, we have to hop off the pier. And then we have to hop to the house. Ma will cut us loose."

I twisted my head and sucked in air. "Right or left?"

"Hop right."

"I'll be in the water!"

"My right. Your left. Ready? One, two, three, *hop!* One, two, three, *hop!*"

It must have taken a half-hour to hop sideways to the house like two crazed frogs escaping from an explosion at the Elmer's glue factory. Uncle Jake trotted along happily, circling our feet and barking, trying to leap at the philosophical fish.

The fishing rod, by this time flying like a flagpole from Bash's back, bounced with each hop. I discovered that if we hopped hard enough, I could get the rod to smack Bash on top of the head. He found that if he hopped hard enough, he could get the trout to flop me in the backside, until it somehow flew up between us and got tangled up there near our armpits.

We saw eye to pit to gills.

———

Aunt Tillie licked her fork one more time and set it on a napkin. "I suspect this trout tastes so good because you hooligans tenderized it all the way to the house."

Uncle Rollie smacked his lips. "You boys want to come fishing with me this Saturday?"

I shuddered. "No thanks. I'd rather do something safe, like ride a giant kite off the grain silo."

Bash nodded. "Or rig the corn picker to launch flying chickens in Superman capes."

I rubbed my shoulder. "Maybe even arm wrestle Mary Jane for free hits. Fishing's way too exciting for us."

Uncle Rollie flicked open the shirt button over his ballooning belly and shook his balding head. "Great oogly booglies. You don't know what you're missing."

Yes, I did. I'd be missing Bash's armpit, for one. And philosophizing. We'd been unwound and cut out of the fish line hours ago. But I still felt all tangled up, twisted and slimy inside. Stupid philosophizing.

Was I lost in globs of pond scum? From what? Lost like

in the woods chasing the fox in the dark? Should I holler for an angel? Chatter at God like Bash and Bonkers?

No! I wasn't lost. Even if I was, I wasn't waiting for a fisherman to hook me. I'd be great once I got away from this Farm of Doom. Just wait.

So why wouldn't the cold, squishy pond scum feeling go away? I hurt.

Help.

Chapter 19

Fair Week Vexations

Whoever called it the "gentle lowing of the cattle" never bunked in a barn with a whole crop of them. There's nothing gentle about a couple hundred cows mooing at midnight.

It was the first full week of August—fair week. Herds of farm animals and flocks of 4-H kids filled the barns on the county fairgrounds. When the fair closed down for the night, a few clusters of kids camped overnight in the barns. Somehow, I'd been "lucky" enough to join them. Oh, joy. I twisted for about the hundredth time inside the tattered sleeping bag rolled out across hay bale beds and clamped the clumpy pillow over my head. "Shut. Up."

"Knock, knock." Oh, great. Not another one. There's nothing gentle about the lowing of several dozen 4-H kids telling dumb jokes while bunked in a barn, either.

"Who's there?" a voice whispered from atop another hay bale. In the storybooks, hay is soft and cushy. Yeah, right. Try rock hard and scratchy.

"Interrupting cow," the first voice answered.

"Interrupting co . . ."

"MOO!"

Giggles and hushed laughter erupted from kids atop hay bales. Cows coughed and bawled. The adult adviser for our 4-H club gurgled and smacked his lips in mid-snore from his lounge chair a ways down the aisle.

Another voice: "Hey, what do you call a cow who just gave birth? De-calf-enated!"

More stifled laughter. I shifted for about the hundredth-and-one time, burrowing further into my sleeping bag, try-ing to fall asleep amid all the lowing in a place that smelled of sawdust, dirt, hay, and cow droppings. Impossible.

But I must have dozed, because suddenly I woke up snort-ing minty foam out my nostrils. Never be the first one to fall asleep when camping in a barn with a pack of 4-Hers. I spat shaving cream as the guys roared with laughter and the cattle lowed a lot.

My dear cousin Bash gasped between guffaws. "It was great! Roy squirted shaving cream onto your palm and Dale tickled your nose with hay until you swatted at it in your sleep. Splat, you got yourself!"

Dave tossed me a rag. "I hear that if you dribble water on a guy's palm while he's sleeping, he'll wake up inside a soaked sleeping bag. Go back to sleep, Ray."

Little Jig jumped to my defense. "No way. We'll be stuck smelling wet sleeping bag."

Dave hooted. "We're in a barn. It already smells. Go back to sleep, Ray."

"Jerks." I rolled off the hay bales and shimmied out of the sleeping bag. Dragging it behind me, I poked my glasses up my nose and stalked out of the barn. I spent the rest of the night scrunched between two rows of wooden bleachers in the show ring, hoping not to roll over and drop beneath them to the sticky milkshake cups and corn dog wrappers below.

So I suppose I was a little crabby the next morning as I watched the Basher, chomping his tongue in concentration, separate the long switch of hair at the end of a Jersey heifer's tail into three even strands. He began braiding it. I stepped back into the sawdust aisle and shot glances around the cow barn. Nobody else seemed to notice the weirdness.

Bash chomped and weaved, chomped and weaved until he held a tight, black braid by its tip with his left hand and reached back with his right. "Gimme the rubber band, Beamer."

I passed over the rubber band I'd been holding. "The county fair is supposed to be fun."

Bash twisted the rubber band until it held the braid in place. "It is fun."

"Uh-huh. Yesterday, you cut the cow's toe nails . . ."

"Hooves."

"*Hooves* . . . with clippers that look like they'd chop up a car. Then you buffed the hooves with shoe polish."

Bash rubbed the red cow's flank with a towel. "Yep."

"This morning before breakfast, you gave her a bath with a hose. You used baby shampoo."

Bash brushed straw from the heifer's leg. "Jerseys have sensitive skin."

"You cleaned her ears with Q-Tips. You trimmed her hair with barber's clippers. You've got baby powder sitting over there and I don't want to know why. Bash, here's a clue . . . *She's a cow!*"

Bash tossed the towel into a trunk, let the lid slam shut and plopped down on it. "Beamer, 4-H judging is tomorrow. Henrietta Herbie's got to look good for the show ring."

Henrietta Herbie is the name he tacked onto the cow, listed as an eight-hundred-pound Jersey heifer. Uncle Rollie thought a twelve-hundred-pound Holstein to be too big for a shrimp like Bash.

I kicked a clump of sawdust. "Fairs are for rides and sausage sandwiches. Instead, we're camped out in a cow barn."

Horses, sheep, goats, rabbits, chickens, pigs, turkeys, llamas, lizards, iguanas, and gerbils crammed other barns and buildings. Bonkers probably had one of every kind of animal on the fairgrounds. The farm kids didn't seem to find anything odd about spending the night in straw-filled pens next to their pigs or turkeys.

I shook my head. "So why are you braiding a cow's tail?"

"When I comb it out tomorrow, her tail will come out all wavy, fluffy, and pretty."

I rocked back. "You did not just say 'fluffy and pretty.'"

Bash jumped up. "Hey, let's take Henrietta Herbie to the show ring and practice." A rope halter tied Henrietta Herbie to a hitching board. Bash slipped the halter off her head. "Hold her around the neck so she doesn't go anywhere."

I hugged my arms around her neck like I was the one going gaga over a goofy cow. Henrietta Herbie stepped backward and I grimaced. Bash dashed to the trunk and came back with a leather lead halter, the cow version of a dog's leash, only it went over her head. He slid the front over Henrietta's nose, pulled the back over her head and behind her ears, and tightened it into place. "Excellent."

Bash led us both to the show barn. "Okay, here's how to show a dairy cow."

Oh, just perfect. Another one of his "teacher" moods.

"Stand there in the middle of the ring like you're the judge. All of us leading cows circle the judge. See, I walk backward so I can see what she's doing."

Yippee.

Bash stepped backward beside Henrietta's head while she strolled forward. "This is why I walked her around the yard the last few weeks. I taught Henny Herb to walk slowly and steadily."

"How about if I yawn?"

Cow Trainer Bash held up the lead strap. "With this hand I jiggle the strap very slowly. Jerseys can get nervous. So I play the chain like a really slow beat box to keep her calm."

"Jerseys, nervous. Bash, DJ. Got it." I pretended to write it down.

"With the other hand, I pet her neck. When I want her to stop, I touch her shoulder like this . . . and she stops."

I wished Bash would stop. But he was right. Henrietta stood still. She did try to lick Bash's right ear with that giant, slobbery tongue.

Bash pointed to the floor. "Her front legs gotta be even, but the back leg closest to the judge should be behind the other rear leg."

"Can't think of anything more exciting than this," I muttered to myself.

"If they're not, we take a step to switch feet. When the judge moves to the other side, I move her feet again. It's posing."

I wrote another imaginary note. "Dollie cow, poses. Bash, dork."

Cow Trainer Bash was in full teacher mode. "I need to keep her head up so her back is straight. If she tries to break into a run, I rein her in, gently rattle the chain and talk softly."

Okay, Bash had a way with animals. A kid who could train a hog to sail a pirate ship or ride a cow to an ice cream stand knows something. I guess.

Bash tossed me the lead strap. "Here, now you try it."

Yikes. "I don't know how to walk a cow."

"Beamer, I just showed you. Here, wrap the strap around your hand and wrist so she can't get away from you. Now walk backward. See, it's fun."

I cooed into Henrietta's ear. I backed up, expecting to trip at any second. I jiggled the chain. It sounded like a ratchet, not a fall-asleep radio station. I held her head up and encouraged her to walk beside me at a slow, steady pace. She was doing it. I couldn't see where we were going, but we were doing this. I could be like Bash.

Cow Trainer Bash patted his back pocket. "Oh, I forgot Henny Herb's curry comb. I'll go get it." And before I could say anything, Bash blasted out of the show barn, tapping Henrietta's flank with what he probably thought was a calming pat as he sped past.

It wasn't calming.

Henrietta froze for two seconds. Then she jumped like a rocking horse in reverse a couple seconds more. I yanked and rattled the chain. It startled her more. Henrietta began to run.

I had a split second to decide which to do—hang on and try to slam on the brakes, or let go and tell Bash which direction I last saw his cow. I let go. I forgot the strap coiled four times around my hand and wrist. It didn't let go of me.

The heifer kicked and bucked and bolted out the show barn much faster than I thought a cow could run. I kicked, bucked and bolted right along behind her, much faster than I thought I could run. *"HENRIETTA HERBIEEEEEEEEEE! LET GO OF MEEEEEEEEEEEE!"*

I flopped and flapped like a rag doll dragged behind a track star cow. The video arcade flashed by. A cluster of wide-eyed teenagers ahead of us scattered as we burst through the ranks. I heard a chorus of yelps as a shower of hot french fries, vinegar and glops of ketchup rained on us. An elephant ear smacked me in the face. Powdered sugar tickled my throat, making me sneeze.

My free hand finally grabbed the strap, and with both hands I tried to yank down, digging in my heels. I skidded along before bouncing down on my rear end then back to my feet, like a fallen water skier skipping across the waves behind a speedboat.

I saw the Scrambler ahead and hoped that Henrietta didn't have any ride tickets. Or that she'd make me ride on the outside where I'd get crushed.

A girl screamed. "Mommy, that cow's doing a pirouette. Can we get a dancing cow too?" She could have this one.

Suddenly, it ended. Henrietta Herbie just stopped. I crashed to my knees, exhausted. A crowd gathered around, clapping and cheering. Somebody yelled, "Hey, cow catcher, you owe me an elephant ear!"

I unwound the lead strap and dropped it. An imprint of the brand name—Swendle—etched my cramped palm. Shaking circulation back into my hand, I growled at the elephant ear guy, "Take hers. Both cow ears. The tail too. The whole cow."

Henrietta stood there, looking thoughtful, chewing her cud, ignoring all the squeals, flashing lights, hiss-bangs of the rides and the growing crowd of people.

Cow Trainer Bash ran up, wedging his way through the crowd. "Ray-Ray Sunbeam Beamer, that was awesome. You shoulda waited for me. I'd have borrowed Dale's Holstein and we coulda put on a real midway rodeo." He tilted his head, studied Henrietta and frowned. "But you shoulda waited until after show day. I just washed Henrietta Herbie. Now she has cotton candy in her hair. And fries."

I wobbled to my feet, poked my glasses up my nose and stomped away. "Yeah. You owe that guy an elephant ear. I gave him your cow. And you stopped calling me that, remember?"

"Ray-Ray. Raymond!" But Bash couldn't keep up. Henrietta decided she needed more time to gaze at the midway. Bash was too small to drag a cow that didn't want to go.

I was tired, angry, embarrassed, and sore. Only two more weeks and my nightmare on Bash's farm would be over. I'd come to the fair for bumper cars and gyros—something normal for a change. I got Bash, pranksters, and Barbie doll cows in track hooves.

I bought a vanilla milkshake at the Holstein Club tent. Then spent all the quarters Uncle Rollie and Aunt Tillie gave us for doing chores on blowing up alien space ships, racing cars, shooting ducks and punching out boxers at the video arcade.

What a few days ago felt like a glob of cold, heavy and squishy pond scum inside was growing into the whole pond, scum and all. Why did Basher find everything so much fun? Most of his stunts were stupid but he kept having a blast. Bash was nothing but a feather-brained numbskull.

A *happy* feather-brained numbskull.

Me, I'm cautious. Smart. Not bad, not like Tommy "The Snot" Snoggins. But outside of his mean tricks, I supposed Tommy wasn't so bad, either. So where did that leave me?

Not bad. Not good. Not happy. Not sad. No fun. Maybe if they let me have my potato chips and comic books back.

But that didn't sound so fun anymore, either. No friends. Just a doofus cousin and his weirdo farm friends.

Well, fine, I could live with that.

I guessed so.

Chapter 20

Fair Week Victory

Shuffling back to the cow barns three hours later, I wandered through the rabbit barn, the poultry barn, and the sheep and swine barn. I didn't want to see my twerpy little cousin and his slappy happy face ever again.

No such luck. In one of the wire sheep pens piled with straw, Bash sat with his back up against one of the wooden corner posts. Another kid sat at the other corner, a lamb sprawled across his lap. The kid scratched the lamb's head. If lambs could purr, this one was doing it.

Before I could duck, Bash looked up from the little red

booklet he held. "Beamer! Good, you found me. Climb over the pen and come on in."

I hesitated. Ah, nuts, why not? I hadn't played with any sheep yet. I clambered into the pen and plopped against a third corner.

Bash nodded at the kid. "This is Georgie. That's his lamb, Mildred."

I reached over to pet the lamb. "Hey."

Georgie didn't look up. "Hi."

A sheep in the next pen pushed his soft nose through as much of the wired squares as he could and nibbled at my shirt. I reached to run my finger over its spongy nose, but it jumped back and scampered to the other side of its pen.

Bash showed me the red booklet. "A church youth group on the midway gave Georgie this little book with Bible verses. I'm helping him read it. It's about farmin' and fishin', you know."

Georgie shrugged at me. I rolled my eyes in agreement, nodding my head toward Bash. The Basher flipped pages in the booklet. "It's about the 'Romans Road to Salvation.' It's how to have your sins forgiven and Jesus in your heart, all from the Bible book of Romans."

I tried to think of a wisecrack about Romans being all Greek to me, but I had nothing.

Soul-Winner Bash leaned into the booklet. "It says the first stop on the road is Romans 3:23, *For all have sinned and fall short of the glory of God.*" He looked up. "Yep. We've all disobeyed God's rules."

I picked up a handful of straw, wondering if I should throw it. "Ha. You're in trouble all the time."

Bash shook his head. "Sin isn't when things go wrong. Sin is when you disobey. You've been told not to, but you do it anyway."

People walking down the aisles of the sheep and swine barn peered in at us. "I think it's one Suffolk lamb and three ewe-yuck goats," one clown said. Bash grinned his goofy smile at them, waved when they walked to the next pen, then stuck his nose back into the book.

"Okay, next stop is Romans 6:23: *'For the wages of sin is death, but the gift of God is eternal life in Christ Jesus our Lord.'*"

Georgie brushed sawdust flecks off Mildred's back. "God wouldn't really let us die. You said before that God is love. That's not love. That's mean."

Bash shook his head. "God is fair. It's like when Ma tells me if I don't clean my room, I can't have ice cream. If I don't clean, she can't give me the ice cream anyway just 'cause she loves me. That wouldn't be fair to my sister Darla, who cleaned up her stuffed bunnies to get ice cream."

Georgie knitted his brows. "Oh."

Bash waved the book. "But see, the gift of God is life. He wants to give it to us."

My turn: "So why doesn't He? If He's so big, why doesn't He just do it and save us the trouble?"

"He doesn't treat us like little kids. We gotta choose. It's like Pops saying, 'Bash, you want this bicycle?' and I don't answer. He wants to give it to me but I won't take it. How stupid is that?"

Pretty stupid.

Bash turned a page. "Stop three on the road is Romans 5:8: *'But God proves His own love for us in that while we were still sinners, Christ died for us!'* See, bad stuff happened and somebody had to pay. That's the God is love part."

"Beamer, remember when we broke that paddle-ball game in Morris's Corner Store?"

I tossed the straw. "*You* broke it. I was trying to duck when you hit me with it."

"Well, we broke it and we had to pay for it, but neither of us had the money. Then Jig reached into his allowance and gave Mary Jane his money to get us out of trouble—'cause Mary Jane woulda given us a whole bunch of trouble."

"You broke the paddle ball."

"Okay, the paddle was in my hand. But it broke when the ball hit your head. Anyway, Jesus said, 'Dad, don't destroy them. I'll pay for it.' And He did, but first, He spent a lot of time on Earth teaching us how to live. 'Cause He knew that once He paid for our sins so we could have life, we'd have to know how to live it."

Georgie scratched Mildred's ears. "So we just take the gift, then?"

Bash flipped another page. "Road stop four, Romans 10:9: *'If you confess with your mouth, 'Jesus is Lord,' and believe in your heart that God raised Him from the dead, you will be saved.'* And Romans 10:13: *'For everyone who calls on the name of the Lord will be saved.'*"

Georgie scratched his own ears. "So I go out into the woods and yell?"

"Nope. Just ask. Grown-ups call it prayer. But it's just talking to God."

"Oh."

More people peered in at us as they wandered through the sheep barn. Why did they have to look? Why did Bash have to be reading Bible stuff out loud in front of everybody?

A big kid leaned over the rail. "Looks comfortable."

Bash grinned. "We got one more corner open."

The big kid laughed and shook his head. I squirmed against the pen post and stared at the lamb's little hooves until the boy moved on.

"All right, then, road sign five, Romans 5:1: *'Therefore, since we have been declared righteous by faith, we have peace with God through our Lord Jesus Christ.'* And Romans 8:1–2: *'Therefore, no . . . no . . .'*"

Bash held the booklet out to me. "Beamer, what's this word?"

I glanced around to make sure no one was looking, then snatched a quick peek at booklet. *"Condemnation."*

"Yeah, that. None of the stuff Ray said, *'now exists for those in Christ Jesus, because the Spirit's law of life in Christ Jesus has set you free from the law of sin and of death.'*"

Georgie shrugged. "Huh?"

Bash grinned. "It means the devil can't call us his bad boys anymore if Jesus lives in us. See, after you tell God your sins and ask Jesus to forgive you and save you from them, and He does, the darkness is gone and you're free!"

I shifted from the sharp edge of the post. "From what? I'd still be me. A loser."

Bash waved the booklet. "Nope. Lookit the next page, Romans 6, verses 6–7: *'For we know that our old self'*—that's the ugly person we used to be—*'was crucified with Him in order that sin's dominion over the body may be ab . . .'* um"— Bash stuck the booklet under my nose.

I winced, then read the word he pointed at. *"Abolished.* It means done away with," I said.

"Thanks. *'. . . abolished, so that we may no longer be enslaved to sin, since a person who has died is freed from sin's claims.'"*

I scratched my head. "Say what? Make some sense, will you?"

Georgie sat up. "I think I get it. We're new. Like little Mildred, here, just a lamb."

Bash nodded. "Maybe that's why they call it being born again."

Georgie's forehead wrinkled. "So what do we do?"

Soul-Winner Bash set the book down. "Let's just bow our heads now and talk to God. Tell Him all the wrong stuff you did, and tell Him you're sorry—but only if you mean it. Ask Him to forgive you and take away the yuckiness inside. Tell Him you won't live that way anymore, because He can help you so you won't."

If it could get rid of the pond scum on my heart . . .

Bash bowed his head. "Dear Jesus . . ."

"Bash!" I yelped. "There are people walking around out here. They'll see us."

"Cool. Everybody needs the Lord."

"I can't pray when people are looking."

Bash started again. "Dear Jesus, can you clear some space for a couple minutes? Beamer and Georgie need to talk to You. Thank you."

Nuts. Now I knew my cousin was nuts. In this crowd . . . Somebody yelled from the other side of the barn. "Hey, a sow over there is giving birth!"

"Let me see!"

"C'mon!"

"Let's go!"

I looked around. People had been walking all around us. Now they were at the other end watching piglets being born. And we were alone.

Weird.

Bash looked up and waved. "Thanks, God, you're the best." Bash turned back to us. "Okay, guys, pray like this: 'Dear Jesus, I'm a sinner. I'm sorry for my sins and for not loving You. Please forgive me. Come into my heart and clean it up. Let me be the cow and you the guy holding the lead halter. Thank you. Amen.'"

Bash finished but Georgie and I kept whispering prayers. I didn't know about Georgie, but I had a lot to talk about. The more I talked to Him—it was like talking to a friend I didn't know I had—the lighter my heart grew. The pond and scum were draining. Crazy, I know. This whole summer had been crazy.

I'd only done stuff like sneak a comic book to bed, copy somebody's homework paper a couple times or lost my temper and said some bad stuff sometimes when somebody was being a real jerk. But it was still wrong. Sin piles up inside, and makes a guy feel rotten.

I wanted a clean life. When I promised Jesus that if He would have me, I'd start living life His way, something jumped inside, like the way Henrietta Herbie ran down the midway. I can't explain it. But I knew it. I was so happy that if I had hold of Henrietta Herbie now, I'd probably outrun her. I could even dance with an eight hundred-pound red-haired, brown-eyed heifer.

Bash punched me in the shoulder. "Cool, cuz! You're free to live. Don't forget to tell Jesus thank you."

I told Him thanks.

Yep, today had been one wild ride through the midway. But I had a feeling that the real ride had just started.

Chapter 21

Secret Agent Skunk

"C'mon, Basher, let's go!" I shouted over my shoulder as we ran toward the woods.

"What's the hurry? And before breakfast."

It was odd seeing Bash running *behind* me for a change. I grinned. "I want to see if we can find that fox's den in the daylight."

"It's not daylight yet. The sun's still yawning."

I'd rolled out of bed even earlier than time for morning chores. Mom and Dad were picking me up in two days. I didn't want anything left undone. Getting to shove Bash out of bed before the rooster woke up for a change, well, that was just an added bonus.

I turned and backpedaled. "The sun will be cutting through the woods by the time we get far enough in."

Bash rubbed away a yawn. "Beamer, you'll be back. We don't have to squeeze all the adventures in at once."

I felt so light and airy inside since that day last week in the barn on the fairgrounds when I let Jesus into my heart. It reminded me of when Bash ran us through the part of the creek with the jagged stone and my sneakers ripped apart— suddenly, I had a lot more room to move around, and the breezes were cooling.

Being saved didn't stop crazy from happening. Being saved made being alive easier because Someone always was there. Now I had Jesus to talk to. Even in the dark, the light was on inside.

I turned and kept running. After a summer on the farm, I could run a lot longer before getting winded. "If we get to the woods before the nighttime animals go to bed for the day, we might find out if Bonkers really saw a fox that night we camped out and got lost in the woods."

Bash trotted beside me now. "Too bad you capsized Look Out Fort in the pond. We could use it to scout the woods. And I could take a nap."

"This afternoon, let's go swimming again. Hey, maybe we can try for some bass this time if you get out the fishing poles!"

"Rods and reels."

"Whatever. And we never built that racecar you wanted to design from grain barrels and trash can wheels."

Bash picked up his pace. "There is that."

I grinned. I used to expect the worst and was disappointed if it didn't happen. That somehow made me crankier, and then things did get worse. Now, I kinda liked the idea of adventure, worse and all. Strands of sunrise tried to haul themselves over the horizon just before we plunged into the darkened woods. It was easier to pick out the animal trail that Bonkers had started us on that moonless night a few weeks earlier when we camped out at the edge of the woods.

Bash threaded a couple bushes where it looked like the trail wound. "Maybe Bonk saw an opossum. It was dark. It could have been a possum."

"Or maybe he saw the elephant our jungle team hoped to spot."

"That's my gag." Bash rubbed sleep from his eyes. "Wait a minute. You're playing. Okay, I'm in. Maybe it was the rhinoceroseseses. C'mon, Ray-Ray Sunbeam Beamer, let's go."

"Stop calling . . . aw, skip it, Bash Tash A-Rash. Don't get left behind!"

I zipped around an oak tree. And put on the brakes. "Yipes!"

Bash smashed into my back. "Why'd you stop?"

"Shh."

Bash tried to peer over my shoulder. "Did we find the rhinoceroseseses?"

"Skunk."

The skunk wandered about fifteen feet in front of us in a patch of clearing. A white line ran from his wide black forehead to the tip of his pointy nose. Two wide white stripes ran the other way down his black, fuzzy back. A bushy black tail with a white center flickered in the air. It looked like it either needed a good brushing or a haircut.

Bash squeezed around my shoulder. "Wow. Is it Bonkers' skunk Buster?"

"It's not fat like Buster. And Buster would have come over to say hello by now."

This skunk had its back mostly to us—not a comfort—as it dug through a mound of leaves and dirt with its sharp little claws. It ignored us. When you have a built-in squirt gun as good as a skunk's, you can ignore a lot.

Bash scratched his ear. "I wonder why it's sneaking around?"

"Maybe he's looking for some bugs to eat or a place to sleep."

"Hmm." Bash chewed on his tongue a few seconds. Then he stepped forward. His eyes fairly jumped with excitement. Morning people don't stay groggy long before exploding awake.

"Maybe he's a secret agent skunk. And he's on a case. I bet he's looking for stolen secret decoder rings. Two rings with big, purple stones in 'em that are really micro-computers. And an agent named, um, Marcus Mad Dog DeLozier Miranda the Sneaky stole 'em and Secret Agent Skunk has to find 'em."

'Maginative people don't stay sane long before exploding with something silly. "But he's a . . ."

The skunk examined the dirt mound, poked at it with his little nose, then clawed some more. Only two days before I'd go home. Not much time for one last adventure. This time, I was going to have fun. This time, it was my turn to make up the game. I wanted to show Bash I'd learned how.

"Why, it *is* a Secret Agent Skunk. But not purple rings. I think a woodland turkey stole something from that fox's den we're looking for. Um, baseball cards."

Bash pondered this. Finally, he nodded his head thoughtfully. "Baseball cards. Hmm. A wild turkey. Okay. That might work. Um . . . oh, I know. The forest has a baseball team called the Laughing Brook Foxes. The fox was in charge of the baseball cards to be passed out to all the little kid foxes."

Yeah, that would do it. I clamped my hands on Bash's shoulders like he was a secret agent in my command and explained the situation. "Only a wild turkey wanted to steal them because he plays for the other forest team, the Turkeys. That weasel Spy Turkey left the foxes with only Wild Woods Gobblers baseballs cards."

"Yeah, Secret Agent Beamer, that's it. So the fox hired Secret Agent Skunk to find where Spy Turkey hid 'em."

I studied the investigating skunk. "We better stand guard."

The skunk didn't find the cards in the dirt mound. He waddled further into the woods on its short legs.

I shoved Secret Agent Bash. "Follow him. He might need our help cracking the case."

"Check."

Off we went, Secret Agent Bash and Secret Agent Beamer providing protection for Secret Agent Skunk. He sometimes walked and sometimes scampered in that skunk waddle. He didn't seem to mind our help, although he didn't stop to thank us, either.

"Probably he doesn't want the Spy Turkey to spot us," Bash said. "So he's keeping cool and not tipping him off to us."

The missing baseball cards weren't in the hollow of a fallen log. They weren't hidden alongside several shrubs the skunk investigated. They weren't stashed behind the moss, which I'm pretty sure wasn't growing on the north side of the tree.

Secret Agent Bash pushed back his baseball cap. "Wow, Spy Turkey's good."

I put up my hand. "Look, Secret Agent Skunk glanced back at us. He's waving at us with his tail."

Bash tugged his cap back down. "Some kinda signal, I bet. I think it means, 'Watch out.'"

"Yeah. We must be getting close."

Secret Agent Skunk stopped again at what looked like it might have been a rabbit hole. He poked his head inside and studied it.

I pressed against a tree and watched. "I wonder if that's it."

Secret Agent Skunk's shoulders disappeared as he pushed further inside the burrow. Then his body slid on through.

His bushy tail flapped a bit just before the hole swallowed him up. Secret Agent Skunk was gone.

Bash pumped his fist. "I think he found it. It must be where Spy Turkey stashed the Laughing Brook Foxes baseball team cards."

"C'mon, Secret Agent Bash. We better move in and keep watch. We can warn him if Spy Turkey comes. Um, wild turkeys are small, aren't they?"

"Bigger'n our chickens. But black and scrawny with skinny, red necks."

"Okay."

We waited. I shuffled a little closer. We waited some more. Bash sidled up beside me.

"What now?" I walked around the burrow to inspect the entrance from all sides.

"Bonkers says skunks like to find burrows or logs to sleep in when the sun comes up."

I dropped to my knees and crawled forward a bit. "So is he done spying for the day?"

Bash crawled up beside me, then scuttled closer to the burrow. "I bet Secret Agent Skunk found the cards and has to guard them until his secret agent team arrives to help."

Bash stuck his head to the hole. "Hey, Secret Agent Skunk! We can help you take the baseball cards back to the foxes."

Secret Agent Skunk didn't answer.

Bash sat down by the hole. "Maybe if we could reach in there, we could drag him and the cards out and be heroes. Then we could take Secret Agent Skunk home to be our pet, like Buster."

Fun is fun, but I saw it was time to do what Mom and Aunt Tillie hoped I'd do when I came out here this summer—talk common sense into Bash.

I sighed as I toed some dirt into the hole. "Your mom would climb a tree and not come down if we brought a skunk home. You'd have to take care of Darla and your dad would have to cook supper. Remember that night your dad cooked? Fried lizards in fly sauce, I think."

"I guess." Bash slumped against a tree.

Finally, Bash was listening to me, the smarter one, and staying out of trouble.

Suddenly, Bash pushed off the tree. "Look, here comes Secret Agent Skunk."

The skunk's triangle face popped into view. He was biting on the stick I'd been poking down the burrow. Well, c'mon, it takes forever to talk sense into the Basher. So while I waited for him to catch on, I figured I'd poke around a bit to check the deepness of the burrow. I dunno, maybe there were secret tunnels and escape routes to thwart Spy Turkey.

Secret Agent Skunk playfully batted at my stick. He crawled out of the hole and made some kind of hissing sound.

Bash dropped to his knees. "He's talking to us. Hi, Secret Agent Skunk. Do you need us to take a message to the Laughing Brook Foxes?"

I scooted beside Secret Agent Bash and held out the stick. "Wanna play some more? C'mon, fella, here it is."

Secret Agent Skunk made some kind of secret snarling noise to tell us how much fun he was having. Then he rounded his body in a "U" shape so that both his front end and back end faced us.

He prepared to deliver a coded message!

"Woo-wee!" Bash choked out as we gagged our way out of the woods.

I coughed and wiped some yellow, misty stuff off my arms. "I just remembered something else different about Bonkers's pet skunk and wild skunks. Wow!"

Bash wheezed. "I thought he'd save that kind of thing for Spy Turkey."

"I think he found the Spy Turkey. Two big turkeys." Bash sniffled and grinned. "Secret Agent Skunk didn't even tell us if he found the stolen baseball cards. Maybe he meant to, but when you threw up, he ran away."

I coughed some more and wiped my eyes, careful to use the arm that hadn't been hit by the yellow mist. Suddenly, it occurred to me—I'd finally got the little twerp back! I told him I'd get him for all the trouble he dragged me into. Only, it happened after I no longer wanted revenge.

I flopped down in the hayfield and burst into laughter. "Keeping you out of trouble is harder than I thought."

Bash shrugged. "Well, it's baths in tomato sauce again. Good thing we had a good crop of tomatoes this year. Ma says that one of these years, we'll get to use some for spaghetti sauce too."

I wiped more tears from my eyes, sneezed and got to my feet. "Country people are weird. But mostly in a good way."

Bash gagged one more time. "Pops probably won't let us in the barn. We smell too bad."

"We smell worse than a dairy barn?"

Bash exploded in snorts and giggles. "Well, yeah. So when are you going home, Beamer?"

"Mom and Dad should be here day after tomorrow. Then we'll start out for home the next day. Yuck, this stuff stinks!"

"You know what, Beamer?"

"What?"

"I bet you get to stay another two weeks."

"What makes you say that?"

"Just a hunch, Beamer. Just a hunch."

Chapter 22

Good-Bye, We Must Be Saying Hello Now

Mom winced when she hugged me. "Raym . . . (cough, cough) . . . You're so thin . . . *Phew!* . . . So tan. You look wonderf . . . *Woo* . . . Raymond, what have . . . (gag) . . . you been into?"

"Hi, Mom." I hugged her again as she tried to push me away.

Across the kitchen, Dad twitched his nose and squinted. "Um, you're looking a little red, Ray."

"It's the tomato sauce. We get to take baths in it."

Bash ran into the kitchen. "Ray-Ray poked a skunk with a stick!"

Mom stepped back again, one hand over her mouth and nose, the other ready to throw a football block on Bash. She narrowed her eyes at me. "Why were you poking a skunk with a stick?"

"Um . . ." I shrugged. It's hard to tell which plans will work and which won't until you dive in. I learned that from watching Bash all summer.

Mom squeezed her nose. "A thtunk! A thtick! Whath were you thtinking?"

Uncle Rollie chuckled. "They weren't. They're boys. No thought cells were harmed in the making of this adventure."

I opened my mouth to protest, then closed it. I figured Uncle Rollie might be right. Instead, I rushed into another subject. "I learned how to swim. Aunt Tillie told us we can swim all day long in the duck pond if we wish. All night too!"

Aunt Tillie shrugged. "I thought it would help."

"Stinky boys!" Darla yelled from her high chair.

Bash narrowed his eyes. "I bet Mary Jane taught her that."

No time to get sidetracked now. I had a whole summer to tell about. "Aunt Tillie's letting us eat all our meals outside at the picnic table. And we get to camp out in a tent too. We would have camped out in our tree house, but it capsized."

Mom started to rub her temple, then grabbed her nose again. "How doth a tree houth capthithe?"

"When we set sail in it, remember? I called you about that. But it capsized. I think the Pirate Pig of the Pond weighed too much."

"The pirate pig? Of the pond?"

"Seriously, Gulliver weighs too much."

"Gulliver? What happened to the pirate pig?"

Basher started pacing. Mom and Dad winced every time he breezed past. "It's simple, Aunt Patti! We built a pirate fleet using Look Out Fort as our flagship, but Gulliver J. McFrederick the Third—that's my riding pig—tipped it over just before Uncle Jake O'Rusty McGillicuddy Jr. saved Beamer from drowning. So I taught him to swim, which is great now that the skunk squirted us. Got it?"

"Raymond drowned? I thought that was another wild tale he made up hoping we'd let him come home early. You know, like when he made up the story about riding a cow in traffic."

"We did! We rode cows all the way to the ice cream stand. And you shoulda seen him dragged down the midway by a cow. My cousin Beamer is the funniest guy I know."

Mom sat down. I would have thought she would have pulled out a chair first, but I guess she was tired. Aunt Tillie rushed over to her. "Now, Patti, it didn't happen quite the way the boys described—"

"Sure it did, Ma. Oh, and Beamer, remember when we wrapped Jig in flypaper and pushed him out the hayloft so he could fly!"

Mom clunked her head back against the wall and stared at the ceiling. "What's a jig in flypaper?"

"Jig Gobnotter. The kid who lives a couple farms over."

Mom rubbed both temples. "You pushed boys out the hayloft? And drowned Raymond?"

"Just one. And he flew. Until he splatted into the manure pile. And Ray-Ray didn't drown. He's right here. You shoulda seen when he put that soup can on his head in church so I could shoot him with my slingshot!"

It was the first time I ever saw that tic in my mom's eye. Dad looked a bit dazed. He turned to Uncle Rollie and opened and closed his mouth a couple of times without anything coming out. Finally, he said, "So, Roly-Poly, how are the crops?"

"Oh, fair to middlin'. I reckon the corn will do okay. If it doesn't, we'll always figure it should have."

"So the boys were active? It doesn't sound like you told us everything that went on this summer."

Uncle Rollie grinned. He pulled out his handkerchief, blew his nose, wadded up the hankie and stuffed it back into his overalls pocket. "Oh, business picked up a bit at the sheriff's office. Ah, not really. Actually, Frankenstein, they thought up a couple stunts that would have done us proud all those summers ago. But they missed a few, like the time we rounded up all those cans of spray paint and sneaked over to Vendetti's sheep farm and . . ."

Uncle Rollie suddenly noticed that Aunt Tillie and Mom were glaring at him. He shrugged and chuckled. "Hey, don't look at me in that tone of voice."

Bash and I nudged each other. Mary Jane Morris had a goat. We'd seen both orange and green touch-up paint on Uncle Rollie's workbench.

Aunt Tillie's glare suddenly whipped full force onto us. "Not on your life. And it will be your life as you know it."

There was something else I hadn't reported in the phone calls home. "Mom, Dad, I've been saving the best part as a surprise for when you got here. I gave my heart to Jesus."

Mom's hand dropped from her nose to her heart. Dad whooshed out a breath like a feed sack fell off his shoulders. I knew they'd been praying hard for me.

"Wonderful!" Mom crawled over and hugged me without flinching—almost—before pushing me away again. She was getting used to the smell.

Dad stretched way forward for a quick, long-distance handshake, jumped back, pinched his nose, and saluted instead. "How'd it happen, son?"

"I wanted to go to heaven. I wanted to love life like Bash and the rest of the kids. I wanted the big blob of pond scum out of me. So after Henrietta Herbie ran me through french fries and an elephant ear, I sat in a barn with Bash and Georgie and Mildred the lamb, and while a pig had piglets, I talked to Jesus."

Dad arched an eyebrow. "Okay, I understood some of that. I think."

Mom wiped her eyes. I thought she'd gotten used to the skunk smell. "I remember how I used to have that cold pond scum sloshing against my heart." Mom didn't seem confused anymore. It's funny how muddled grown-ups' minds can get, and then suddenly they'll surprise you by latching onto something you didn't explain.

I dropped my head and scuffed a sneaker on the kitchen tile. "Anyway, I'm sorry for not listening to you guys, and not cleaning my room when you told me to, and all the times I was bad just because I was angry, and all the other stuff."

"Welcome to the family, Raymond," Mom said quietly.

"But I've always been part of the family. Unless I was adopted. Was I adopted?"

Dad nodded. "Yep. Just now. You were born to us, but now you're adopted into God's family too."

I tried to figure this out. "I guess that makes sense. More than Bash calling the Bible a farming and fishing book."

Uncle Rollie rubbed his chin. "Well, Jesus does use a lot of farm talk. My favorite is Mark 4:30–32: *"And He said, How can we illustrate the kingdom of God, or what parable can we use to describe it? It's like a mustard seed that, when sown in the soil, is smaller than all the seeds on the ground. And when sown, it comes up and grows taller than all the vegetables, and produces large branches, so that the birds of the sky can nest in its shade."*

Dad clapped Uncle Rollie on the back. "Roly-Poly, you harvested a crop for me. Thank you, and thank the Lord."

I couldn't figure out what they were talking about. I just knew that I'd miss this nutty farm and yes, even Cousin Bash. He did teach me to swim, after all. And to enjoy adventure, even if it sometimes kinda stinks.

"Can I stay again next summer?"

Bash jumped up. "Yeah, can he? We haven't built our grain barrel racecar yet."

Mom blinked a couple times and turned to Dad. "Frank, aren't you going to tell them?"

Dad snapped his fingers. "Oh, yeah. The firm offered me a transfer to the Ohio office. We'd be back in the neighborhood."

Move to Ohio? Live near this weirdo farm? Would that mean . . . ? "Could I take Amy to the fair next year?"

Mom smiled. "Amy? Raymond, did you find yourself a little friend? Did you buy her cotton candy?"

"Mommmm, don't be gross."

Bash jumped in. "Nope. He walked around the fair with Henrietta Herbie, and she's a real cow."

"Sebastian, it's not nice to call a young lady a cow."

I slapped my forehead. "Mom, she is a cow. A Jersey. And Amy's a calf. But she will be a cow."

"Oh."

Bash paced a circle in the middle of the kitchen. The grown-ups scrunched their noses every time he breezed by them. "And Beamer saved her life. He ruined some dumb, ol' quilt, but he saved her life!"

"I didn't ruin it. Amy did. And you're the one who ran it to the barn!"

"You wrapped it around her!"

"Boys!" Mom and Aunt Tillie chorused.

Dad took over. "Anyway, yes, Ray, if we take this move, you could visit as often as you like as long as it's okay with Uncle Rollie and Aunt Tillie."

"And maybe . . ." Mom wiped another tear from her eye and gagged just slightly. "Maybe we could just leave you here in the meantime and not have you stuffed in the car with us for nine hours all the way back to Virginia to pack up the house."

Bash paced faster. He did kinda stink. "That would be so cool. There's so much more we could do. Are you sure we can't spray paint Mary Jane's goat?"

Aunt Tillie's eye ticked. "Nicholas . . ." Aunt Tillie tapped Mom's arm. "I could send both boys back with you to help pack. This place needs a chance to air out."

Bash hooted. "We could go surfing in the ocean. I could pet sharks."

I stomped my foot. "Aren't we forgetting something? How'd I end up out here in the first place? You prayed me out here. Shouldn't we ask God now what's best?"

Dad shuffled close enough to put his arm around me and wrinkled his nose. "Raymond, you're learning. We have prayed over it. We want you to do so too."

"I bet it's yes. Let's pray now. Besides, Amy needs me to help raise her or Bash will give her back that stupid long name."

"It wasn't stupid, it was distinguished."

Mom cut in. "Anyway, we could spend all the holidays together."

Bash rubbed his hands together. "April Fool's Day is my favorite. Well, Christmas, then April Fool's Day. I've got some good ones planned. The cows are gonna give chocolate milk. You wait and see."

Aunt Tillie sputtered. "How are the . . . What plans? No. No, I don't want to know. Stay calm, Tillie, stay calm . . ."

Even as we bowed our heads for prayer, I noticed Aunt Tillie's nervous eye tic winding up for takeoff.

Bash and the Chicken Coop Caper
(Spring 2014)

Chapter 1

Snow Crazy

I perched atop the chicken coop and gulped puffs of frigid air. This was insane.

"Bash, we'll shoot off this roof at a thousand miles per hour, hurtle down the snowdrift mountain, smash through the maple tree, and blast our extreme sail-powered super-board supersleds to supersmithereens."

My crackpot cousin bobbed his ski-masked head. "It'll be *awesome*."

"You think getting killed is *awesome*?"

Sebastian "Bash" Hinglehobb, my third cousin twice removed—but not far enough to prevent avalanches of disaster—swished his sled along a stretch of slick roof slope. "Chill, Beamer. If we crash and croak, we'll slide uphill all the way to heaven. Why worry?"

"Why? *Why?*" My head be-bopped so much that the wool scarf tucked under the edges of my glasses dropped from my face. Ice crinkles crackled inside my nose. "I'll tell you why. Because we might accidentally live. All our bones will be broken, but your mom will make us clean the barn anyway. I'll drag myself along the stinky, gooey floor by my good elbow, pulling a wheelbarrow full of cow droppings with my teeth. I don't even want to think how I'll get the stuff into the wheelbarrow. *That's why.*"

Bash shaded his eyes against the miles of snow sparkling like millions of snow cones. "You worry too much, Ray-Ray Sunbeam Beamer."

"Stop calling me that." I stomped my boot. "*Extreme, sail-powered superboard supersleds*. This has got to be your stupidest idea yet."

But the sooner we got it over with, the sooner I'd be inside with a mug of hot chocolate. I shivered. "Help me rig the sail."

"All right, Beamer. Prepare to have a blast." Bash chunked his sled into the two feet of snow on the roof and high-stepped toward me.

I rolled my eyes. Can eyeballs freeze solid? "Mashing all my bones in a sledding disaster sounds more like an explosion than a blast."

Bash strung pillowcase sails from masts built of rake handles and tomato stakes. I glanced over my shoulder at the other side of the chicken coop. I hated looking down. There was no snowdrift on that side, just a drop-off. A long, dizzy drop-off plunging far, far down into mounds of freezing, frigid . . . I squinted. Were those . . .?

I tapped Bash on his coat sleeve. "Whose footprints are those?"

Bash scanned the trail through the drifts. "Ma's, probably. She collects the eggs early, before they freeze."

"No, *we* collect the eggs, during both morning and evening chores, remember? Aunt Tillie said that was our job. And those aren't our tracks. Basher, I think somebody ducked into your chicken coop."

Bash knotted baling twine onto the corners of a pillowcase sail. "Why? We already got the eggs." He tugged at the twine to make sure the string held. "Maybe Pops needed something in there. Who cares? C'mon, let's get this other sail on."

I peeked down again at the single set of tracks already drifting over in sweeping gusts of wind. They didn't look like Uncle Rollie's footprints, but I'd never looked at his from the chicken coop roof before. I'd never been on top of the chicken coop before. Until the screaming blizzard dumped snow everywhere and blew it into a white ramp as tall as the eaves, we couldn't reach the roof. Not without a ladder. I hate ladders.

"You sure you mom won't care that we used pillowcases for sails?"

"She was too excited to get us out of the house. Didja notice how she set our coats and boots by the door?"

We'd been crammed inside a big ol' farmhouse for three days while snowstorms howled, pretty much ever since Mom and Dad dropped me off Friday. By breakfast time today, Aunt Tillie's crazy eye tic flapped so fast, it threatened to cool off the fried eggs before she got them to the table. "Out, out, out. Go build a snowman or something. Anything."

Fine with me. We'd been stuck playing Candyland with Bash's three-year-old sister Darla, who made up her own rules. One more game of Candyland and I'd scream like, well, like the blizzard.

Now I wobbled atop the chicken coop roof. A wind gust whooshing with all the warmth of Popsicles packed in ice cubes blew my collar open and bit down my back. "Let's go play Candyland with Darla."

"Stop being a baby. This'll be awesome." Bash was shorter, skinnier, and younger than me—eleven, which made him kind of stupid still. I'd turn twelve next month, three months before his birthday. Since I was older, I tried to keep him out of trouble with my smarter brains.

But January blizzards in northeast Ohio freeze brains.

Chief Engineer Bash dug a hammer out of one deep snow coat pocket, and nails and brackets out of the other. He mounted the rake handle masts to our two plastic sleds, his a blue toboggan style with curled up front end, mine an orange saucer like an upside down Frisbee. "I bet no one's ever rocketed off a chicken coop roof on sail-powered super-board supersled."

I pulled off my mittens, shook them against the shock of refrigerator breath, and finished rigging my sail. "I bet no one else would be crazy enough." We were about to get extreme.

Extremely stupid.

Then I spotted the polar bear.

Parent Connection

Remember:

A thief comes only to steal and to kill and to destroy. I have come so that they may have life and have it in abundance. —John 10:10

Read:

In Matthew 13:1-9, Jesus tells one of those farming stories that Bash is always talking about. It's a story about a farmer who plants on three different types of soil, but only one type of soil grows an abundant crop. Read verses 18-23 to see exactly what type of soil—and what kind of person—that is. Whether you're a farmer or a fisher or a kid looking for adventure, Jesus has promised us life in abundance. But it's up to us to tend the soil.

Think:

1. Raymond is always thinking that he's smarter than Bash. Do you think it's true? Why?
2. Raymond's parents are Christians, and Raymond goes to church. Why do you think it is Bash who is able to lead Raymond to become a Christian?

3. How do the three types of soils relate to Bash and Raymond? What type of "soils" do you see in this story?
4. How would Jesus describe your "soil," your ability to hear God's Word?
5. What can you do to be a better farmer, to have better soil where God's Word can grow abundantly?

Do:

Make a Farmin' and Fishin' Book

1. Get or make a blank notebook. (Make one by stapling down the center of a stack of several sheets of paper then folding in half on the staples.)
2. Title the front cover "My Farming and Fishing Book." Decorate or illustrate the cover.
3. As you read and hear farming and fishing stories in the Bible, add them to your notebook. Write the stories in your own words and illustrate them.
4. To get started, you can look back at Chapter 17 where Bash lists several examples.
5. The next time you're "philosophizing" or just wondering about God's place in your life, take out your Farming and Fishing Book and see what God has to say.

Jesus came to fish for men and
to tend the soils of our hearts.

Will you help Him?

A NEW SERIES FROM
accomplished writer and film director **BILL MYERS**

Twin siblings Jake and Jennifer have just lost their mother and are not thrilled about moving to Israel to stay with their seldom seen archaeologist dad. They don't yet understand how "all things work together for good to those who love God." But they will when a machine their father invented points them to the Truth.

Available Fall 2013

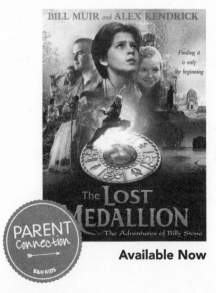

A story of lost treasure and adventure... and of discovering the power of the One who created us all.

The son of an archaeologist finds the lost medallion his father had been seeking and is transported back in time with his best friend for an adventure that will change his life forever.

Available Now

EVERY *little* **WORD MATTERS**™
BHKidsBuzz.com